Jimi & Isaac 3a:
The Mars Mission

Phil Rink

Summary:

Jimi and Isaac are rock stars. They're also epic heroes, intellectuals, soccer players, loving sons, and students in awe of Lipstick, their science teacher. They tell fart jokes and they'd like to have a little lettuce on their sandwiches at lunch. They are wise and foolish, sublime and earthy. They are middle school boys.

Introverted Jimi and brilliant but obnoxious Isaac pester their billionaire buddy Ash Berg into letting them "jazz up" his space expedition. Ash plays along, knowing they will fail and learn from their failure. Issac prefers to make a limited but credible effort and claim a limited but credible victory. Jimi wants more – but good help is hard to find.

For Teachers and Helicopter Parents:
26,000 words.
Flesch Reading Ease: 87.4%
Flesch-Kincade Grade Level: 3.8.

Lots of ideas to discuss.

To Leo.
Because he knows it is important to be resilient.

Chapter 1:
Jam

I don't think the rich guy was buying what Isaac was selling.

"Come on, Mr. Berg" Isaac said, as he adjusted the top cymbal on his high-hat. "Let me be your astronaut. NASA used to send chimps to space, and I'm way smarter than a chimp."

"*Way* smarter?" said Mr. Berg, plugging the guitar cord into his amp. "Maybe. But we have a strict rule at my company: no middle school boys in space. Ask me again once you get your driver's license."

Isaac laughed and hit his drum sticks together with his arms over his head (one, two, one-two-three-four), then rolled into a really cool syncopated groove. Mr. Berg dropped in with a nice A-minor blues shuffle and

I found a simple counterpoint on my saxophone. Then Dad filled it all in with another screaming guitar lead. When Dad talks he is so quiet you can hardly even hear him, but when he plays his guitar he's a whole different guy. Mr. Berg took the lead for the second twelve measures. He had been taking guitar lessons from my father for over a year now and was pretty decent.

Usually, I get to solo on the third time through, but instead of playing a turn-around Dad closed it off with one of his fancy chord sequences. Bummer.

Isaac started in again. "I know I'm right on this," he said, "every government in the world sends adults into space. It's boring. But if you send a kid, people will notice. Every nerd in the world will grow up wanting to work for you."

"Leave him alone," I said. "Too much talking." Dad laughed a little. "Besides," I said, "Mr. Berg's not in it for the fame. He's in it for the money." Then I started a song I really like because the saxophone gets the melody. Dad joined me right away. Mr. Berg followed along, watching Dad's hands to get the chord changes. Isaac just stuck out his lower lip and played the beat on the kick drum, with one crash cymbal on every forth beat. What a baby.

Isaac was talking again by the time the last note died. "OK, then, how about maybe Jimi and me can do a project for your spacecraft, like one of those tiny micro-gravity cockroach mating experiments that totally revolutionizes the micro-gravity cockroach breeding industry."

Dad snorted a little and un-hooked his guitar strap. "That's enough for me," he said. "See you next week, Ash?" Ash is Mr. Berg's name. Dad put his guitar in a stand and headed upstairs.

"Yeah, Jim," said Mr. Berg. My dad is Jim like short for James, but my name is Jimi like the greatest guitar player ever in the whole world Jimi Hendrix. I was probably bred as a name donor.

Mr. Berg packed his guitar and sat down. It was hard to remember that he was one of the richest guys ever, sitting there in his torn blue jeans and T-shirt on what had to be the nastiest basement sofa in the world. The sofa was okay when we bought it at a garage sale four years ago, but then we got a puppy that tore the corners off all the cushions. The puppy had to go live on a farm after that. Mom says the sofa is just one big plaid stain. "Hey Isaac," he said, finally. "Why don't you make a toy spacecraft with a parachute? We can throw it out the window right after we re-enter the atmosphere. Whoever finds it will get a free dining room set."

"You know, Mr. Berg," I said. "Orbiting the earth is pretty boring. It wouldn't hurt to jazz it up a little."

"Yeah," said Isaac. "Jazz it up a little. That's where we come in. Jimi and Isaac, Rocket Jazzers." Then he played a little buh-duh-bum thing on his drums.

"Look you guys," said Mr. Berg. "Orbiting the earth may seem easy and boring to you, but it's pretty hard for a private company without any government support. That's why they set up this contest. The first company to orbit a man around the earth gets a contract to launch satellites for a new world-wide communication system. We walk, then we jog, then we run the race. In that order."

"So walk," said Isaac. "But let us put a little snap in your step. A little wobble in your wander. A little shimmy in your..."

"How about a robotic explorer?" I asked. "Normal stuff. Just make a little radio-controlled car thing and run it all over the moon. We can put your logo on the back and have video cameras and sensors and maybe a plaque with pictures of people and maybe a message of peace..."

"Too stupid." interrupted Isaac. "Like you said, normal. You need to think abnormal, like me. We send stuff into orbit every week. TV satellites, phone satellites, weather satellites, war satellites, cat satellites, dog satellites, gerbil satellites, it's old news, man! Who cares? It's just an old science fiction movie. Big deal!" Isaac was waving his arms around. "We need a Mars explorer." Mr. Berg just smiled and leaned back on the sofa with his eyes closed. Isaac didn't notice. "Mars is way bigger than the moon, so there's lots of unknown areas. They'll probably name a crater named after us."

"Yeah, Mr. Berg! Mars!" I said. "Mars is cool. It's just like our soccer coach tells us all the time: 'Go Big or Go Home, Boys! Go Big or Go Home!'" I gave Isaac a thumbs-up. Sometimes he had some pretty good ideas.

Nobody moved. Mr. Berg looked like he was fake sleeping. Isaac shrugged and put his sticks on the tom drum and headed out the sliding glass door. "Come over tomorrow morning, Jimi. We need to finish that history timeline for Monday."

There was another long silence while I put my saxophone in its case. I was worried that Mr. Berg might really be asleep. He was slouching on the sofa with his legs stretched out and his head laid back. Finally he opened his eyes and leaned forward. "You think a Mars probe is easy?" I shrugged my shoulders. "Okay, I'm calling your bluff. Here's what you do. You build a probe that will go from earth orbit to Mars, taking pictures along the way. It doesn't need to do anything else – that's hard enough. It's got to fit inside two five-gallon buckets stuck together end-to-end, understand? And it's got to weight less than 100 pounds."

I looked up and nodded like I agreed with him, but really I was trying to remember how big buckets were. He was staring right through my eyeballs at the back of my head. He didn't look mad, just really serious.

"Come on, Jimi. It's time for you guys to figure out the difference between talking about something and doing something. You're OK, but Isaac is getting a big mouth."

Isaac has had a big mouth for a long time. I thought everyone knew that.

"You're going to need a budget," he continued. He rolled to his feet, reached into his jeans pocket and pulled out a wad of money. Without even counting it, he held it out towards me. It was as big as my fist. "If you can build it for this and get it to me by the first of

June, I'll put it on my rocket and you'll be the first kids to send a probe to Mars."

We both just stood there Nobody moved.

"I thought you said it was easy." More standing.

"Take it," he said, "see how good you are. You'll never know what you can do until you try. Go big or go home, right?"

This time, he smiled. I reached out and took the money.

Chapter 2:
Jimi and Isaac Design the Probe

My first Saturday as a rocket scientist started out pretty normal. Mom and Dad were up early and out cleaning up the garden. All that's left are some carrots and a bunch of dead tomato plants. Two weeks ago Isaac and I got in a ton of trouble for throwing all the old rotten tomatoes against the fence. You can still see the stains even though Isaac and I scrubbed it for over an hour. Well, I scrubbed. Isaac said that the stains added "texture" to an otherwise boring fence, and then he called my mom a fascist, which is like the worst kind of dictator. I told Isaac to go home and I cleaned the fence by myself.

Anyway, I got up and made myself some instant oatmeal. Then my sister Janis started screaming from her room that I was making too much noise. Apparently the microwave goes "ding" too loud for her highness. "Shut up and go back to sleep," I told her.

She stormed into the kitchen and poured my oatmeal into the garbage disposal. While she was ranting about noise and destroying my breakfast the phone rang. Janis stopped screaming at me and answered the phone all nicey-nice, in case it was a boy: "Peterson house, Janis speaking."

She listened for a short time. "No, little boy, He isn't here. He's dead." And then she bashed the phone down, gave me a dirty look, and went to her room and slammed the door.

I figured the "little boy" was Isaac and tried to call him back, but Janis was on the phone in her room and wouldn't get off. I listened in a little but it was just some other girl and they were talking about who was kissing who and stuff. Finally Janis heard me breathing on the phone and threatened to kill me some more. I wouldn't want my only sister to have to spend her life in jail so I slid into my jeans and T-shirt from yesterday and rode my bike over to Isaac's.

When I got there Isaac's dad was just finished making pancakes for Isaac and his mom, but he broke out the box of mix and made me a stack too. I ate them with extra syrup. While I was eating Isaac talked about Mr. Berg and his company and the spacecraft he was building.

"I don't think we're supposed to talk about that," I said between mouthfuls. "I think it's private."

"Don't worry, Jimi," his mom told me, "We won't tell anyone. But you're right; you boys shouldn't be talking about Mr. Berg's business. It's a form of gossip, and we expect better from you."

I wanted to point out that it was her son, not me, that was gossiping, but she never sees anything wrong with Isaac.

"If Berg doesn't want us to talk about his projects he shouldn't talk about them with you two," Isaac's dad said. "At the university we're under unbelievable pressure, but you'll never see me discussing my work with a bunch of adolescents." Then he started telling this really long story about another professor that hadn't cleaned his laboratory in over two years and was going to have to get going if he didn't want a reprimand (a reprimand is like getting officially yelled at). I didn't get it, but Isaac's mom thought it was a good story, because she started talking about a graduate student she worked with who was doing really good work but just wouldn't write any reports. I already knew that a graduate student was a person who goes to school for a job, but doesn't get paid very much. I don't know how you can go to school and not write reports. I guess that was her point.

We finished our pancakes and slid away while his parents were discussing this professor who wears the same clothes every day. I smelled my shirt and it seemed fine, so I figured they didn't notice. Isaac was sniffing his shirt, too.

When we got to his room I showed Isaac the wad of money Mr. Berg gave me. "Cool," he said, "this will be a piece of cake. We'll get my dad to help and we'll have this thing done by Halloween. Then," he said, eyeing the roll of money, "we take the leftovers and spend the winter in Hawaii."

"No way," I told him, "if you tell your dad about the money, he'll tell my dad. If my dad hears about the money he'll make me give it back. Besides, Mr. Berg wants me, and I think us, to do it. He wants us to see how good we are. We do this by ourselves."

Isaac looked at me with his mouth open.

"You're the one who said it was easy," I said. "You're the one that's built model rockets for practically your whole life. You're the one who made fun of Mr. Berg's space program."

"I didn't make fun of it", Isaac said, "I said it was boring."

I just waited. I could tell that Isaac was thinking.

"Okay," he said, shrugging his shoulders. He sat at his computer and typed "Mars probe" into a search engine.

We spent hours looking at information on rockets and Mars and orbits and thrusters and video cameras and radio antennas and orbits and all kinds of space stuff. We made up a huge shopping list for things we needed, and then we spent a lot of time arguing about what color to paint the rocket.

Right before dinner we remembered we were supposed to make our timeline for history class. Isaac did some research and I got out some colored pencils and we made the fastest timeline ever. It wasn't any good, but it was good enough.

The next day we talked Janis into driving us into town to the model rocket and hobby store. She gave us a funny look when she saw us carrying all the stuff we bought.

"It's for a school project," I said in the car on the way to Isaac's house.

"That's right," said Isaac, "My dad got a grant to study space education so he's having us try his ideas." I just about exploded trying not to laugh.

"Your dad teaches chemistry, Isick." Janis was on to us.

"I meant my mom. Middle School Space Physics is the thing. Space Physics, Physical Space, you know, Spacitude."

"Uh-huh," she nodded. "Just be safe with that rocket. Those big motors you got can really do some damage."

We had a bunch of the largest motors they made. We also had the biggest rocket kit we could find. It built a rocket almost as tall as we were.

"We'll be fine," I told her. "But don't go scaring Mom, okay?"

She looked at me through her big round hippie sunglasses. "If you leave me out of it, I'll leave them out of it, at least for the time being. Just don't get dead."

At Isaac's house we snuck all the rocket parts into the house and up to his room. His parents don't usually care what we do, but we figured the less we had to explain the better.

I put the rocket model together while Isaac did some more research on the Internet. He found some little video cameras that radio the picture back to the base station. We figured we didn't need the cameras for now so we just made up some balls of duct tape that were about the same size as the cameras and put two of them in the nose of the rocket. The rocket was built out of cardboard tubes, like paper towel tubes, so it was easy to cut the holes.

I had the rocket almost completely built when I remembered that Mr. Berg said that the whole probe had to fit into two five gallon buckets, end to end. Isaac found two buckets in the garage from when they painted their house and brought them up to his room. Five gallons sounded like big buckets, but our rocket model was way longer than the two put together.

"Just cut it in half!" Isaac said. "Most of the rocket is just empty tube anyway."

"Yeah," I said, "but they must have had a reason to design it that way."

"Sure they had a reason," Isaac said. If the rocket is twice as long they can charge twice as much. Just cut out the middle and reattach the top lower down." I didn't move. "Gimme that!"

Isaac grabbed the nearly finished rocket kit from me and cut the body tube right in half. He then cut the top part off just behind where we were going to mount the cameras. "Hand me that tape," he said, pointing.

I didn't move. "Don't use tape," I said, "it will be too heavy. Make a nice connection like the kit comes with."

He looked at me with one eye closed and the other one bugged way out. Isaac called it his "stink-eye." Then he grabbed the tape himself. "Chill out. We'll try it this way, and we'll do a better job on the finished one for the rich guy." His tape job was pretty sloppy but it seemed strong enough.

"Okay," said Isaac, "now for the improvements."

"What do you mean?"

"Mars is a lot farther away than you think, my simple-thinking friend. If we're going to get this thing there in our lifetime we're going to need a lot more thrust." He started fitting extra rocket engines around the bottom of the rocket. "See," he said, "just like the old Russian rockets. When their original rocket needed more power, they just strapped on more engines. Simple and reliable. Looks good to me, comrade."

He ended up with five extra engines on the base of the rocket, all attached with more layers of tape. I checked the instruction sheet that came with the rocket kit. It had a pre-launch checklist which seemed pretty basic, except for one thing. "Hey Isaac, it says here to check the stability of the rocket by tying a string on at the balance point, then swing it around my head in a circle and make sure it points forward."

Isaac finished with the tape, stood up and looked around his room. "Well, there's no room to swing it here, and if we do it outside my parents will want to know what we're doing. I say we skip that step." Then he started putting the launch stand together.

I was pretty tired of arguing and it was almost time for me to get home. "Okay, then. Can we launch tomorrow after school?

"Yeah," he answered, not looking up from the launcher. "Tomorrow."

Chapter 3:
The Test Fire Fails

Isaac stood and looked into the sky, slowly turning until he had turned all the way around. It was one of those amazing fall days where the sky was blue all the way to the mountains, and even though it was kind of cold the sun was really bright.

I gave up. "OK. Now what are you doing?"

"Looking for airplanes. I don't want to shoot any down. Safety first, you know."

This made sense to me so I scanned the sky, too.

"Looks clear," I said. "What's next?"

"We added so much power to this thing that it might shoot into the jet stream. The wind up there blows about three hundred miles an hour." Isaac was talking to me like I was four years old, as usual. "If the parachute opens while our rocket is that high it will drift miles and miles before it comes down. I'm cutting holes in the parachute so the rocket will fall faster."

I watched Isaac slash the red and white plastic parachute, then pack what was left into the nose of the rocket. He stuffed an igniter, which is like a little electrical match, into the opening on the bottom of each of the motors we had taped around the base of the rocket, and then he slid the rocket over the long metal rod on the launch pad.

Isaac took a small plastic box from his backpack, unwound the black wires that were wrapped around it, and started making connections. "The long wires go to the igniters so we can get way far from the rocket, and the short wires go to the battery once everything else is hooked up."

"OK, Jimi. You do the countdown and I'll light it off."

"Come on, Isaac," I said, "Mr. Berg put me in charge. I should fire the rocket."

Isaac didn't move. He just sat there looking at me.

I tried again: "Give me the controller, Isaac." Nothing. Arguing with Isaac is the biggest waste of time there is in the world.

"All right," I said. "Ten, nine, eight, seven," I counted dramatically, "six, five, four, three, two, one..."

At "one," Isaac pushed the button on the control box. By the time I said "zero," it was all over. There was a huge zipping noise and a big cloud of white smoke from the launch pad. The rocket got about six feet high before it started flipping end over end like crazy. It looked like fireworks except bigger and faster and not pretty. Three of the taped-on rocket engines tore away from the main rocket and flew off on their own, spitting out smoke in a tight spiral of death. The top of the rocket finally ended up stuck into the ground three feet from my feet.

"Cool," Isaac said.

"Yeah, cool," I echoed. Not cool.

Chapter 4:
Isaac Moves On

We didn't even clean up the mess. We just collected the launch equipment and our backpacks and rode our bikes home without much talking. It was pretty discouraging.

I missed two Friday jam sessions with Mr. Berg because we had soccer games, and by the time I finally had a Friday afternoon free Dad said Mr. Berg got too busy at work and had quit taking guitar lessons.

I kind of stopped working on the probe after that. I really didn't know what to do next and I guess it was easier to just go to soccer practice and do my homework. Besides, I was depending on Isaac for ideas and he was definitely gone—I didn't see him all Fall after the launch. I don't know if he was just having too much fun with jazz band, or he was embarrassed because the rocket messed up, or what. I never asked him, either.

Then this really bad thing happened. Maybe it wasn't such a big deal, but it scared me. A lot.

I started stealing Mr. Berg's money. I mean, it wasn't stealing because he gave it to me. But I did spend it on things that didn't have anything to do with the Mars probe. So, yeah, I guess I stole it. Mostly I bought junk. I took a little to buy a juice at lunch. Then I bought pizza instead of eating my sandwich. Then I bought some really nice reeds for my saxophone. See, the really good reeds sound better and are easier to play, and somehow I figured that it was okay to use the money for reeds because…well, I don't know. It all seems pretty stupid now. But I ended up taking about three months' allowance worth out of my "budget."

The week before Thanksgiving I stopped Isaac in the hall at school. "I need to give Mr. Berg his money back."

"No way," Isaac told me. "That's your money. He paid you to try, and you tried, and it didn't work. It's your money."

"We didn't try very hard," I said. "One rocket and some tape. It tried to kill us and we quit!"

"Look, this happens all the time. Somebody gets a grant, and they try something out, and it doesn't work, and they keep the money. My mom says that the real money is in writing grant applications. Nobody cares very much if it works."

Jimi & Isaac 3a:

For some reason this got me really mad and I started yelling at Isaac about how that was dishonest and nasty, and I hope he doesn't treat his friends that way, and how he shouldn't ever treat me that way. I guess I got pretty loud. That's when the Lipstick showed up.

Chapter 5:
The Lipstick

Mrs. Lipner is the best science teacher in our school. Maybe she's the best teacher in our school. She's really nice and pretty smart, but mostly she doesn't let us get away with a lot of crap in class so we tend to learn. A lot. But she is also tall and she has bright red hair and she paints her lips bright red so everyone calls her Lipstick.

"So what's the fuss?" Lipstick asked.

"Jimi's building a space probe." Isaac said. I gave him a look to shut him up because it was supposed to be a secret, but he stuck his tongue out at me. Like he was three years old or something. "It's going to Mars."

Mrs. Lipner got this great big smile. "That's terrific! I just got approval this morning to hold the science fair and you boys are already working on a project – wonderful! Now tell me about the spaceship!"

Isaac decided that this was a good time to be helpful. "It's not a spaceship—anyone can make one of those. Jimi is making a Mars probe to be launched from an orbiter. It will fly all the way to Mars on its own sending back video and all kinds of science information." While I stood there and glared at him he told her all about the probe and rockets and video cameras. At least he didn't say anything about Mr. Berg and the money.

"Fantastic," she said. "Mr. Peterson, I'll give out entry forms in class tomorrow and I expect you to have yours turned in this week. That will give you eight weeks to finish your project. We'll have the judging right after mid-winter break."

"Great," I mumbled.

She gave me a big smile. I could see all her great big white teeth framed by her great big red lips. "Great," she said.

Chapter 6:
A New Design

So now I couldn't quit working on the Mars probe. I had two adults that wanted me to do it and I told them I would do it so I figured I better do it. I filled out the science-fair entry form and then my parents had to sign it. Now everyone knew what I was doing, except only Mr. Ash and Isaac knew about the money. I had two months until the school science fair to finish the probe. Soccer season was almost over, too, so now I would have more time to work on it. Even though soccer isn't a subject, it's still pretty important.

Isaac was no help at all. I mean he helped, but in his own special way that made you wish he wouldn't help. He'd say my ideas were stupid then leave to go talk to his jazz band friends.

Lipstick was excited about the whole thing. After I turned in my entry form, she asked me to stay after school.

"This looks like quite a project, Jimi."

"Yeah," I answered. It was. Quite a project.

"You wrote on the bottom of your entry form that you are going to be showing a Mars probe." She looked at me over the top of the paper and I nodded. "You should probably put 'A Model of a Mars Probe' or 'A Plan for a Mars Probe,' just to be more correct."

"No," I said, "I'm building the entire thing. It will be completely working and everything so somebody could use it after the contest." She just kept looking at me. "If, you know, somebody liked it and had a spaceship to launch it from and stuff."

"Okay, Jimi, you may have it your way." She looked at me a little longer. "Just make sure it's safe, please. This will be our first science fair at this school and I don't want it to be our last."

Then we talked for a while longer about how to present the probe, how the display should look and what kind of information I should include. She said I need an overall drawing showing the parts and what they do.

"I don't need drawings and descriptions," I said, "I'll just bring the whole thing and people can see for themselves how it works."

"Jimi, you're in middle school now." Oh, great. A speech. "You are here to learn and part of that process is that you must demonstrate what you've learned.

Science-fair entries are judged on the quality of the presentation as well as the quality of the idea. You need drawings, pictures, a display board, and a written report as well as a model of your spacecraft. Do you understand?" I nodded my head. "Good. Why don't you make up some rough sketches of your ideas, and then maybe I can help you put your display and report together." I nodded again and we agreed that I'd bring sketches in the next day. Suddenly this Mars probe business was a lot of work.

Chapter 7:
Help from Teacher

That night I meant to work on the probe design sketches for Ms. Lipner but Dad wanted to play some music, then I had to do dishes, and then there was this great show on TV. I didn't get my math homework done either. Science was after lunch, though, so I made up some sketches while I ate my sandwich.

"You haven't shown a lot of detail on these sketches, Mr. Peterson," she said. "That's fine for now but for the science fair you'll want to show details of everything. You need an overview of the entire space probe and then detail drawings or models of each system."

"There's just one system," I told her. "The Mars probe. I launch it off of someone else's rocket."

"Think of it this way, Jimi. A car has a drive system that makes it move, a steering system that controls the direction, and a braking system that makes it stop. All the systems together make one car."

"Yeah, but…."

"No yeah-buts. Do this project right and I think you'll do well in the science fair. The judges will like the ambition you've shown by tackling such a large problem."

We worked together for ten minutes after school and came up with four systems on the probe: a rocket-motor system, a steering system, a camera system, and a radio system. Mrs. Lipner made me draw out a picture of the probe showing where I thought each system should be. I drew a picture of a pretty standard rocket with the rocket motors in the back, and the camera in the front. I figured we'd just move the fins to steer the probe and I used a wire sticking out of the rocket tube for a radio antenna. Lipstick and I agreed that was a pretty good start.

"Fins, huh?" said Isaac when I showed him the drawing. "That's pretty stupid, even for a saxophone player." I just looked at him, waiting for the rest of it. "They call it space for a reason. There's no air there, nothing for the fins to push on. Fins only work in air. Once it's in space they don't do anything. You must be the worst Mars probe builder in the world." I didn't bother to point out that we put fins on the first rocket we built, and they seemed like a good idea at the time.

"That antenna is stupid, too. This is supposed to be a space probe, not an old TV set."

"So what should it look like?" I asked.

"Look, Jimi," Isaac said, picking up his backpack, "I don't have time to save you on this one. You'll have to figure this out for yourself. I'm busy with my own stuff and my parents said they'll take me to Europe this summer if I get good grades, so you are on your own." Then he threw his backpack over his shoulder and ran to his mom's car. "Good luck, space boy!" he yelled as they drove away.

I unlocked my bike and rode home.

During dinner this really weird thing happened. Janis talked to me like a human being.

"I heard that you're in the science fair," she said as she mixed her corn and mashed potatoes together. "That's cool. Ben and I are going to be judges."

Ben is this guy that Janis had been hanging around with for a couple of years. He's pretty cool, and way smart. He was almost as smart as Janis. But they weren't dating. They just did things. Sometimes they did them together. No dates. Janis was real clear on that.

"Yeah," I said, "maybe. It looks like it's harder than I thought, though. I don't know if I'll do it."

"It's only hard if you make it hard, sweetie," said my mom. Isaac says Mom is a flower child. She has really long hair that she always wears in a ponytail, she wears big loose skirts and T-shirts, and she gives massages to people for her job. She sees some things differently than most people. But she's really nice to people and lots of them ask her advice, so I guess maybe different is okay.

"Well Mom, it's just that I don't know much about spaceships but I already told Lipstick, I mean Ms. Lipner, that I was going to build a Mars probe for the fair." Dad made a little chuckling noise and stood up, then cleared his dishes into the kitchen.

"Maybe your sister can help you," Mom said. "She's read a book or two in her life."

Janis made a face at Mom, but she was smiling, too. Janis knows she's smart but she always likes hearing about it from other people. "Come on, Jimi," she said, "it's a middle-school science fair—how hard can it be?"

I couldn't tell everyone that I was building a real Mars probe, not just a science-fair project. "Yeah, I guess you're right. But you're going to be a judge, so you can't help me."

"They won't let me judge my little brother anyway. In fact, I don't think I'll judge anyone in your grade, so if the Boy Genius needs help I can help him, too."

"Well," I said. This could get really uncomfortable. I really didn't want to talk about Isaac and his bigger and better attitude right now. "I don't think he'll be in the fair. He seems pretty busy these days."

Mom gave me a serious, sad look, then started to clear the table. "You two go talk for a while."

I showed Janis my sketch of the probe then told her what Isaac had said about fins and antennas. "No problem," she said. "He just proves that you can be a jerk and be right. Here," she gave me a couple of books on space travel, "why don't you look through these books and see what you think." I think they were written back in the old days when people were just starting to go to space. They had pictures of these really small satellites and a few pictures of spacemen on the moon. The rockets looked just like a rocket should look, but the satellites and the thing that landed on the moon weren't smooth or long or anything. They looked like something I would build, all messy and stuck together and jumbly.

"Since there's no air in space, there's no air resistance, so spacecraft don't have to be streamlined," Janis told me. "Also, there is much less gravity in space, so they don't have to be as strong. They just have to survive the rocket launch from earth. Then they'll usually be strong enough to do whatever else they need to do. The spacecraft can be light and use really small rockets once they're in space."

"Cool," I said. "Thanks." Cool, I thought, and took the books to my room. I had some reading to do.

Chapter 8:
The Science Fair

I didn't even recognize Ben at first. He was wearing a tie and clean tan pants and he had brushed his hair. He and two other guys from high school were my judges at the science fair.

There were three other projects in my grade besides mine. Ben and the other two guys didn't spend much time at all talking to the girl that built the vinegar-and-baking-soda volcano. They spent a lot of time talking and laughing with the guy that put the video camera on his radio-controlled car. He called it a "mobile sensor" and had lots of video of him chasing his dog around and running into parked cars. The girl next to me had a lot of calculations and a lot of graphs to show the best way to grow grass seeds in a dark room using different lights and different ways of watering and different fertilizer and something else I don't remember. I didn't see the point of her experiment—our lawn has always been outside. Ben and the other judges seemed pretty impressed, though.

Then it was my turn. I had a huge cardboard stand with my drawing of the probe showing the whole thing, and smaller drawings showing the different systems. Mostly, though, I had the probe itself. Some of it was pretty rough, since I'd put it together that morning with blue masking tape, but overall I thought it was pretty good. Parts of the model were real, like I had real rocket motors to drive the probe through space, but I didn't know what real steering rockets would look like or where to get them, so instead I had some of the cardboard tubes from the inside of toilet-paper rolls taped on where I would use controllable rockets to steer the probe to Mars. I had a real wireless video camera that radioed the picture back to my "earth station," and I had an empty cardboard box taped on that said, "controls." I didn't know what to really use there, either.

Ben asked some really good questions about the steering system. "It all depends on the center of gravity," I told him. "If you push through the center of gravity, it moves sideways. If you push off to the side, it turns." The center of gravity is like the balance point. "It's important that the fuel tank is on the center of gravity, otherwise the probe will steer differently when the tank is empty."

That impressed the other two guys, but then they said some mean stuff about it all being faked up and not planned out. "It's pretty good for a middle-school kid," Ben said, "and it's good that he tried something hard." The other guys shut up a little. I didn't feel real good when they left.

Anyway, the grass-growing girl won, I placed second, and the radio-controlled-car guy placed third. Grass girl won a dinner at a pretty good restaurant and she would get to grow her grass at the state science fair in two months. I didn't even really know who she was. I'd seen her at school a few times but I'd never heard her talk and wasn't sure she was even taking any math or science classes. It was pretty depressing. It made me kind of sick to my stomach.

"Good job," Ben told me later. "I like what you did."

"Thanks. But I didn't win."

"So what—you should be proud," he said. "Why don't you keep on working on it and enter it again next year?"

"Yeah, that sounds good," I said. "But actually…I'd kind of like to finish it now, you know, while I'm thinking about it. I just don't know anything about controls or antennas or…." There were a lot of things I didn't know about.

"Maybe we can fix that," Ben said. "I know a guy that knows all about things like this. Why don't you and I go see him tomorrow after school?"

"Tomorrow?" I mumbled. "Well…okay. How much of this stuff should I bring?" I waved my hand at the model and drawings I'd done for the fair.

"Don't bring anything," Ben said. "First you meet, then you talk, then you help out a little, then you ask questions. Wilson James is not someone you just ask."

Chapter 9:
Wilson James: Rocket Scientist,
TV Repairman

"Jimi, huh? Wow. A name like that, I'll bet you're killer with the ladies." Wilson James was old, maybe 30 or 35. He had long frizzy hair and his belly stretched out the front of his work-shirt, which was a blue knit polo with a worn-out collar and "WJ Electronics" embroidered on the pocket. He wore a baseball hat that said *No Bad Days* on the front and *One Day at a Time* across the back. He didn't look like much to me, but Wilson James was Ben's expert.

"I did science fair in high school. Won it every year. Almost won state in my junior year, but the judge was too dumb to understand my report. He picked some nimrod's orchid-growing project over the short-wave radio I built. I bet the flowers never talked to anybody behind the Iron Curtain! I was talking to a commie in Czechoslovakia at the height of the Cold War!" Wilson James looked at me because I laughed a little during his story. He finished his diet orange soda, crushed the can and threw it at a trashcan in the corner, and got another one from a small refrigerator under the workbench. "What?"

"Oh, I'm sorry," I said. "It's just that I got beat by a girl that grew grass indoors."

"Hydroponics," Ben said. "It was pretty cool, actually."

"Last I heard, it was illegal to grow grass indoors," Wilson James snarled. "You don't smoke dope, do you?" He looked at each of us in turn. We both shook our heads no. "Good, there's no quicker way to get stupid than smoking dope. That is something I know about. There's a reason a man like me is running a tiny shop like this instead of my own electronics company —and dope is at the bottom of it. Dope and booze, booze and dope. No better way to get stupid. Dig a big stupid hole, and spend the rest of your life digging your big stupid self out of it."

I started to explain that she was growing grass like a lawn not grass like drugs, but Wilson James had already moved on.

"So what are you two doing here? I'm pretty busy, and you can't have any parts. I don't have any spare anything around here."

"No, Mr. James, we don't need parts," Ben started, "but we could use some advice. Jimi wants to finish his Mars probe design, and there are some areas where he doesn't know what to do next."

"Yeah, and what about you, Ben? Why are you here?

"I'm just helping Jimi—we're friends—well, his sister and I...."

"I get it, I get it," Wilson James interrupted. "There's always a girl. Yep. There's always a girl."

This was followed by a pretty long silence. I certainly had no idea what to do or say so I tried really hard not to move or look at anybody.

"Okay," Wilson James finally said. "I'm in. Jimi, you show up here tomorrow after school and we'll talk. Actually, you'll work and I'll talk. There's no such thing as a free lunch, you know." He gave me a real serious look. "You do know that, don't you? No free lunch."

I knew he wasn't talking about food but I decided to make a little joke. "I'll eat on the way over," I said.

He finished his diet orange soda and tossed the can in the trash. "We'll do fine," he said, getting another soda. "See you tomorrow."

The next day was Friday. When I showed up at his shop the door was locked and there was a 'CLOSED' sign on the door, so I bailed and went home. Nobody works on Friday night, anyway. I was busy with my mom on Monday because I had to get some pants that were long enough to cover my socks because Janis said I looked like a dork when my pants were too short. I guess she was right, about the pants I mean. Mom and I went to the thrift store and I got three pairs of jeans that were all in pretty good shape. She says there's no point in buying me new clothes when I'm growing so fast. She said that I can have new pants when my wife buys them for me. Whatever.

Anyway, I went to Wilson James' shop again on Tuesday. It was open this time.

"Mr. Jimi. Good to see you. Where were you last week?"

"Uhh, I came by on Friday, but the shop was closed. The door was locked and stuff."

"And stuff, huh? I just had to close up for a minute or two. You should have waited around. Now you've wasted almost a week. I thought you said this project was important."

"Well, it is important…I really need to make it work," I said, reaching for my backpack. "Do you want to see the diagrams I've made? I've got separate diagrams for the drive system, the naviga…."

"Not yet, my young assistant," said Wilson James. "First things first. No free lunch, remember?" I nodded my head. "You take this trash bag and collect all the garbage around here, and then you separate it— aluminum cans go in the blue bin, paper in the red bin, and the rest goes in the garbage can out back. Got it?" I nodded my head again. "Then get to work! I thought you said this project was important!"

I made three passes around his shop picking garbage off the floor and the workbenches. Every time I thought I was done he pointed out something I missed. I was having a really hard time deciding what was trash and what was valuable equipment. Finally, "I'm done."

Wilson James took a slow look around the shop. "That'll do for now," he said. "Let's see how it looks out back." He led me to the alley where the huge trash bins were. "I see a lot of aluminum cans in the trash, here. I told you to put those in the blue bin, right?"

I took a look into the bin. I had to stand on a bar on the side to really see in. Sure enough, there was a big pile of diet orange soda cans in the bottom of the bin. "I didn't put those there," I said. "I even separated some out from the trashcan in the shop. I put every can I found in the blue bin."

"Look kid, if you want my help you need to learn one thing. You'll never get anywhere blaming other people for your problems. Get this can situation straightened out, then come see me and we'll get started."

Well, there wasn't much I could say to that. I had to climb all the way into the trash bin to get the extra cans out. By the time I was done I barely had time to bike home in time for dinner. Mom was real strict about dinnertime, and, since I still hadn't told them that I was really building a real Mars probe for Mr. Berg, I really didn't want to explain where I was.

"I need to go home now," I told Wilson James. "I can't come tomorrow or the next day, either, so I guess I'll see you on Friday?"

"Friday is a no-go, young genius. I am leaving early for the weekend. You need to strike while the iron is hot. You need to make hay while the sun shines. You need to…." He must have noticed that I was starting to walk out. "I'll see you next week, Mr. Jimi. Next week will be good."

On Monday I got to the shop as soon after school as I could, but I had messed up on a math test and had to talk to my teacher after school.

"Spaceboy! Good to see you, even if you are late. Get this place cleaned up so we can fix your space thing."

Unbelievable. I guess Wilson James thought he had a slave now. I almost left and went home, but I looked around and saw that he hadn't made much of a mess since I was last there. "Okay," I said, and started putting the diet orange soda cans into the blue bin, the paper into the red bin, and the trash in the trash bin outside. It only took a few minutes but by the time I was done Wilson James was gone. The front door was still unlocked, and the "OPEN" sign was still lit, so I knew he was around somewhere. I sat on a stool at the workbench next to somebody's microwave oven and waited. There was a bunch of food stuck to the inside of the microwave like they hadn't cleaned it in years. Maybe that's why it needed fixing.

After 20 minutes, Wilson James came back in the front door. "Sorry about that, Jimi. A friend came by— my old sponsor. Checking up on me, I guess."

I didn't know what he was talking about. I just grabbed my backpack and pulled out the plans for the Mars probe.

"You're in middle school?" asked Wilson James. I nodded yes. "That's when I started smoking weed. You don't smoke, do you?" I shook my head no. "Well, don't start. Don't start. Don't start." There was a long pause. Finally I opened my drawings and pushed them across the workbench at Wilson James.

"Right here is the part I really need help…."

"I imagine there's still a lot of drugs in the schools." Wilson James said it like a statement, not a question. I guess he was really talking to himself. "Would you say that more kids smoke, or more kids drink?" This time he really was looking at me. "I really don't know," I said. "My friends don't do either. Most of the kids that do stuff like that just hang out with each other. They don't talk to me much."

Wilson James sat back and crossed his arms, staring at me. When he crossed his arms, it pulled the bottom of his shirt up and I could see his belly button. It had hair in it. "Good, good. That's real good. Not for them, but good for you."

There was another long silence. It looked like I wasn't going to get any help today, either.

Finally, Wilson James uncrossed his arms, stood up, walked over to his little refrigerator, and grabbed a diet orange soda. "Let's get to work," he said as he opened the can.

Chapter 10:
Plans Change

Wilson James really did know a lot. We talked for about an hour and I came home with a bunch of notes he wrote on my drawings, plus five other pages of notes, plus catalogs for video and radio parts. He even had this really cool idea of using a video camera to aim the probe by watching Mars and steering the probe so that the probe was always pointed right at it. He said that's how they steer guided missiles. He also said that when I ordered stuff to have it shipped to his shop and he gave me a credit card number to use. I just had to pay him back when I picked things up. That was pretty cool.

The next couple of weeks went pretty fast. I had soccer practice every night after school plus homework to do, but I read through the catalogs I got from Wilson James and made out a list of things to order. I almost ordered everything on the list, but I double-checked how much it would all cost and it was too much money. Way too much money. So I went through the list again and decided to do just one system at a time. I decided to start with the control system.

I ended up getting some controls that were made for model airplanes and I got a bunch of big rocket motors for propulsion and small rocket motors for steering. Wilson James' idea was to steer the rocket by using a bunch of small rocket motors aimed in all different directions. He said to just fire a rocket that was pointed away from the direction I wanted to go, and then it would push the probe in the right direction. That seemed like a pretty good idea, too, as long as I didn't run out of "steering" rocket fuel before the probe got to Mars. Wilson James said that was no big deal—I just had to get close and then the gravity of Mars would pull the probe in. "A crash landing is guaranteed," he said. "It's like water going down a drain."

He also said that I only need the propulsion motors at the start, to get the probe moving towards Mars. "Space is empty," he said. "You just get the thing moving, and it will keep going. In fact, once you get closer to Mars the probe will just keep going faster and faster until it hits because Mars will pull the probe towards itself." More of that water and drain idea, I guess.

Then this thing happened.

Lipstick asked me to stay after class, which was no big deal because sometimes I help her at lunch or after school when she has to set up the classroom to do experiments and demonstrations. "Mr. Peterson," she said, "I received some very important news today. Do you think that you can put your model of the Mars probe back together in two weeks?"

"I...I suppose so," I said. She didn't know I was still working on it, so I suppose she thought that I tore it apart after the contest.

"Good," she said, "then you'll need to do that. Our first place winner has had to leave our school under some, umm, strange circumstances, and you will be representing our school at the state science fair. Congratulations, Mr. Peterson."

Well, that was weird.

After practice I rushed over to Wilson James' to tell him the new plan. "The grass grower had to leave school, huh?" He turned to his workbench and picked up a newspaper. "Anybody you know?" he asked, pointing at a picture on the front page. The picture was of a man and a lady being walked out of their house by the police. Their hands were behind their backs. I suppose they were wearing handcuffs. In the door of the house behind them was the science-fair girl. A police lady was standing next to her. The girl had this empty look on her face. Under the picture it said: "MARIJUANA FARMERS ARRESTED."

"Wow," I said. "She was growing drugs?"

"Her parents were growing drugs. Lots and lots of drugs. Now they will go to jail. They will go to jail for a very, very long time. It says here..." Wilson James stopped to read the article. "'...the girl has gone to live with her aunt.' Looks like you will be the only one that gets any good from this otherwise horrific mess." Wilson James read the article all the way through. "Look, grasshopper," he said, "why don't you go home and tell your parents your good news. Don't worry too much about this...." he waved his hand over the paper. "You had nothing to do with it. Maybe it will work out the best for this girl, too. You just never know."

I said "'bye" and left. Wilson James locked the door and turned off his sign as I got on my bike. He was pretty bummed out.

Ben and Janis were already at my house when I got home. Supposedly they were doing a "project" together. Yeah, right. Anyway, Ben already knew about the science fair, so Janis already knew, and they both told my Dad, and when Mom got home they told her. I didn't get to tell anybody.

Mom was pretty excited, though. "Wow, another scientist in our family," she said. "I always thought that you would be an artist like your father. I guess we better start a college fund for you, too."

"I'm still an artist, Mom," I protested. "It's not like I'm quitting band or not practicing. Besides, lots of great scientists are musicians."

"Yeah," said Ben, "and some of the greatest music of all is practically math. We've been studying Bach in music theory, and…."

Janis cut him off. "Yeah, yeah. Sure. Algebra, calculus, melody, geometry, tempo. All the same. No doubt. Slam-dunk. Anyway, Jimi, you've got a lot of work to do if you're going to get that mess cleaned up in two weeks. The state science fair is a lot different than the tiny thing at your school. You need to make all new posters, and show a lot more detail, and you need to get a suit with a tie, and you'll…."

Then Mom cut her off and put her arm around me. "There's lots of time for problems later. Right now I think that we can spend this evening, or at least this dinner, just being proud of our own fresh rocket scientist."

Chapter 11.
The Big Show

Janis was right. I had a lot of work to do.

First I had to re-do my sketches to show all the changes that Wilson James had suggested. Then I had to figure out what changes to make to my Mars probe. I couldn't get everything done before the competition and Lipstick said it was okay to fake some stuff in as long as I didn't pretend that it was real and that I knew what would really go on the probe. I also wrote a report on the whole project. I included space diagrams and a history of the design, including the bad ideas from before. That was another suggestion from the Lipstick. I decided to leave out the details of the first messed-up nearly fatal launch, though, because I didn't want to get

Isaac or me in trouble. I just wrote: "An early test launch didn't work as planned."

I put all my sketches into a folder with the report. Then I re-drew some of the sketches larger to make three posters that made a wall behind my model. I colored the posters in with markers so that each system was a different color. Mom even took an afternoon off to take me shopping. Not at the thrift store. Mom said I was all ankles and wrists. My old shoes still fit but Mom wanted me to wear new shoes to match my new clothes. I tried on some fancy black shoes but Mom said I should just get some nicer sneakers so I could wear them to school after this thing was over. She did get me some black socks, though. They looked pretty weird with the sneaks.

The state contest was on a Friday. Dad drove me to school before the sun came up and we picked up the Lipstick and drove into the state capitol. I think Dad and Lipstick talked, but I was mostly asleep. I woke up when Dad parked the car in the basement of some huge building. Dad carried the Mars probe and Lipstick carried the posters up to the meeting hall. I carried the report. We had to take an elevator. We checked in and found the table where my project went and set everything up. Then we went back down the elevator and had breakfast in a restaurant in the same building. By the time we got back upstairs to where the contest was, the place was a mess. There were about a thousand kids there and about three thousand teachers and parents and judges. The judges all wore red ribbons on

Jimi & Isaac 3a:

their chests and most were wearing suits. Dad was really kind off freaking out. I didn't feel very good, either. There were too many people and there was too much going on. Luckily the Lipstick was cool. "Come with me, you two," she said. "We'll go get a hot chocolate." I wasn't really thirsty since we just had breakfast that was really the second breakfast I'd had since I ate a little before we left the house, but I did what she said. Anything to get away from the crowd.

Lipstick led us out of the big room and down a hallway to a little space they had set up with some chairs and tables and there was a great big window that looked out over the city. We were way in the air and I could see the river and the cars and the highway and a ton of people. "Why don't you save this table for us while I find the drinks," Lipstick said, pulling out a chair for me to sit on. I was so busy staring out the window I didn't hear her at first but finally I sat down. Dad sat across from me. He was staring out the window, too.

"Wow," he said. His eyes were pretty big. "This is wild." Finally he blinked and looked at me. "You know what, though? You belong here…you deserve to be here."

"There is no doubt about it," said Lipstick as she appeared out of nowhere from behind me, putting three cups of hot chocolate on the table. "No doubt about it. Your school is proud of you, Jimi, and I am proud of you."

50

"I'm proud of you, too," Dad said. Then he turned back to the window and stopped blinking again.

We sat quietly and drank our hot chocolate. Then it was time to go back to the judging and the crowds. Dad reminded me to go the bathroom. That was a good idea.

The contest was different, to say the least. Different from school, different from my friends, different from anything I've ever seen on TV or heard about or read about or even thought about.

First of all there were a lot of kids around, and they weren't like the kids at school. I mean, they were like the kids at school, but not like the kids you normally talk about when you talk about kids at school. These kids were kind of nerdy, but not in a bad way. They talked about things and had done stuff that I'd never thought a kid could do. A few kids wrote their own video games. Lots of kids built solar water heaters or solar battery chargers or solar-powered model cars. One kid built a nuclear reactor–powered car; only the nuclear reactor was just a model because he said it was too expensive to get real nuclear fuel.

Second of all, the adults that were hanging around all acted really weird. They were mostly parents and teachers but they treated the kids like they were the most important people there. Most of them read my nametag so they could use my name and then asked me really serious questions like: "Will you fly your probe to Mars, Jimi?" and "Have you picked a launch date, Mr. Peterson?" I don't think they were kidding around. Nobody told anybody to shut up all day.

The judges were…well, I don't know what the judges were. They moved around in groups of three interviewing the kids in the age group they were judging. The middle school kids were spread all around this huge room with high-school and elementary-school kids mixed in. I wasn't sure where the other middle school kids were. My judges showed up while I was talking to the high-school kid next to me. He had this huge aquarium thing showing how bacteria can make oil by eating garbage. Apparently the bacteria eat ground-up plants and poop out oil and gas. His project smelled a little.

"Mr. Peterson!" A great big old-guy judge with a smiley-face tie tapped me on the shoulder right when the bacteria oil guy next door was telling me about lighting cow farts. I got a little disoriented.

"Yes, sir," I finally answered.

He introduced himself and the two other judges and I shook their hands. I don't remember their names.

"Please explain your project—it looks like you've designed a spacecraft of some sort."

"Yes, sir, it's a probe. A Mars probe," I said, surprised that he didn't know that from the huge MARS PROBE writing on the top of each of my posters.

"Well, why don't you tell us about your work," he said. The judge behind the other two, who I guess was the youngest one, opened a little folder and got ready to take notes. Smiley-tie was looking at my posters, and the third judge was a lady in a blue suit that was all stretched out at the buttons. She looked right at me and smiled. Like a teacher, I guess, only really interested, not fake interested.

I started with the model and showed them the different systems in the probe, pointing to the poster for each system while I described it. I told them about using a video camera to help aim the rocket, and how it didn't have fins because there wasn't any air in space to make the fins work. There was some confusion for a while because the young guy and the suit lady didn't understand that the probe was launched from a ship that was already in space. The smiley-tie guy finally explained it to them and got it all straightened out.

I got all done and stopped. The young guy finished taking notes and looked up. All three of them were looking at me. Straight at me.

Finally I remembered. Lipstick told me to ask about questions. "Do you have any questions?" I asked. That's what they were waiting for. Blue-suit lady smiled a little.

The young guy had one. "How long will it take to get to Mars?"

I had no idea. Nothing. I looked at my posters for a while. "A few years ago, Mars was only 43 million miles away from Earth. That was pretty close. On average, we are about 140 million miles from Mars." They knew I was reading my posters, but I didn't know what else to do.

He tried again. "How fast do you think your rocket will go?" He gave me an encouraging smile. Mr. Smiley-tie frowned and crossed his arms.

"I don't know," I said. "As it gets closer to Mars, the gravity will pull the probe in faster and faster, like it's falling down a hole. So the probe will be going pretty fast when it hits."

"Does it matter how long it takes?" Smiley-tie was kind of grumpy, now. Blue-suit lady frowned at him, looked at me, and then smiled a little.

"No, not really," I said, "eventually it will get there, and then it will send back some pretty cool pictures I think."

"Unless your batteries are dead and your camera doesn't work anymore. Of course it matters. Those little rocket motors won't be enough. But that's okay, the video transmitter doesn't have enough power to reach Earth from Mars anyway, and the guidance system won't work. Let's remember it's just a kid's science fair." Smiley-tie was definitely grumpy now. He looked at his watch. "Let's keep moving!"

He shook my hand and thanked me for showing my project. "Well done," said blue-suit lady, and she left to catch up. The young guy was still looking over my posters.

"I like this," he said. "You've done a good job. Remember that you can add to it and enter again next year, so keep working on it."

"You keep telling me I'm stupid and I'll keep making it stupider," I said to him, but of course I didn't really say that out loud. I said "Thank you," and shook his hand. He smiled at me and kind of punched me in the shoulder a little when I didn't smile back.

I was pretty down after that, but the day got better. When the judges were done the exhibitors walked around and talked to each other. A lot of other kids were upset, too. I guess the judges asked a lot of hard questions. Dad and Lipstick came and found me for lunch. I had a good roast-beef sandwich with this watery gravy to dip it in and then after lunch they had an awards ceremony. I won fourth place in the middle-school category. That was the lowest prize they awarded. Still, there were like 30 middle school kids there, so I did pretty well. The oily ooze guy next to me actually won the high-school category, which meant he got to go to the national competition.

After lunch they opened the show up so parents and sisters and brothers and other people could come through and see all the different exhibits. That was pretty great. Three girls from a school in another part of the state kept hanging around my display and calling me a rocket scientist. They said I was pretty cute for a nerd. I told them I was actually kind of ugly for a musician, which made them giggle and then run off somewhere.

I didn't spend too much time looking at other projects, though. I was pretty tired. I barely remember helping Lipstick and Dad load the display and the model in the back of the car, and I don't remember climbing into bed that night. I guess I missed supper.

Chapter 12:
Fame

Even though I didn't think it was that big a deal to get fourth place in the state science fair, everybody else did. For a while.

On Monday they had an assembly at school, just for me. They got the whole school into the gymnasium, just like there was a basketball game or something. The band even played for a while until everybody had a chance to sit down. I didn't get to play because I had to sit on a folding chair in the middle of the basketball court between the school principal and Ms. Lipner. The principal said hello and how nice everyone looked and told everyone to be quiet and respectful. Lipstick made a little speech about the importance of science, and the importance of creative thinking, and the importance of stick-to-it-ness, which I don't think is a word. Then she gave me the plaque that was the fourth place award from the Science Fair. I was supposed to make a little speech, but I didn't know what to say, so I just said "Thank you." I mumbled when I said it. That was pretty goofy. Everyone clapped for a little while then left the gym and went back to class.

Afterwards a guy from the newspaper took a picture of Lipstick handing me the plaque, which was actually the second time she handed me the plaque and the third time I had been handed the plaque, and then after the assembly he asked me a few questions. I told him that I had some help building the probe but that I was the only one that had worked on the whole thing. He asked if my Dad built it for me. I laughed and told him that my Dad is a guitar player. I told him that I played saxophone and soccer. Then the newspaper guy asked if my mother built it for me. I told him Mom wasn't a builder. He stared at me for a while after that. I guess he didn't believe kids built things. "OK, Mister, umm…" he looked at his notes, "…Peterson. Jimi Peterson, right?" he said. I spelled it for him. Then he closed his notebook.

"His name is Jimi!" Isaac interrupted, suddenly appearing from behind me, "and I'm Isaac. Isaac Farmersuit. Jimi is the front man, and I do all the work. Jimi makes it feel good, and Isaac does the science, get it?" Newspaper Guy opened his notebook again.

"So you built the Mars probe?" Newspaper Guy asked Isaac.

"Most of it," said Isaac. "Jimi is a little slow sometimes, so I have to step in or stuff never gets done."

I didn't say anything. My mouth didn't seem to work. It just hung open. I may have even drooled a little. At least I didn't pass out. I don't think I passed out. Maybe I passed out. After about an hour I could finally talk again. "Isaac helped me with the first rocket last fall," I said. "He hasn't even seen the model I entered in the science fair."

Newspaper Guy wrote a little in his notebook. "Isaac...?" He said, looking over his glasses.

"Farmer. Isaac Farmer. Me and Jimi are a team, have been since forever. Jimi...Isaac." He talked real slow while Newspaper Guy wrote.

I couldn't believe it. "And what part of the, umm..." he looked at his notes, "...Mars probe did you build, Mr. Farmer?"

"I'm just Isaac. Mr. Farmer is my father." Newspaper guy was writing like mad, now. "That's like a joke. My Dad is Professor Farmer, the famous chemistry professor. My mom is Professor Farmer, the famous physics professor. I'm not famous, you know, yet." Then Isaac actually winked at Newspaper Guy. I almost fell down. "I built the parts of the Mars probe that aren't made out of tape." Then I fell down. Well, I didn't fall down, but I did go sit on the bottom seat of the bleachers. This was really too much. Newspaper Guy even took Isaac's picture.

The article was in the newspaper the next day. It was worse than anything. The headline was "Local Team

Places Fourth in State Science Fair" and then under it, in smaller letters, it said "Only One Student Gets Award." There was the picture of Lipstick giving me the plaque and then a larger picture of Isaac that said "The Unsung Hero" underneath. I didn't really read the article. I felt kind of sick to my stomach. I just threw the paper out before my parents saw it. I didn't want to talk about it.

Actually, I didn't feel very well for a week or so. I didn't get my homework done, I was nasty to my friends, and I really messed up on a vocabulary test. The teacher actually called my mom at dinnertime to see if I was sick or something. During spaghetti. With meat sauce and really good bread and almost no vegetables.

"No, Mom, I'm fine," I told her. "I guess I just wasn't ready for the test. I'm sorry."

"Come here," she said, and she gave me a big hug. Mom gives the best hugs ever, by the way. She doesn't let go until you hug her back. This time she had to wait for a while, but I finally got the message. I also noticed that my chin was over her shoulder this time. I guess I've grown since my last hug.

"Thanks, Mom," I said. "I just got caught up in the science fair. I'll get back into my schoolwork right away."

"Let Janis help you," Dad said. "You two can talk to each other now that you are both certified geniuses."

"One contest doesn't make him a genius, Dad. At least he shows a little promise. I'll see if I can stir the mush in his head." Janis smiled at me. It was weird.

Janis did help me with my math, a little, but she knew what the problem was. "Did you beat the crap out of Isaac?" she asked. "That boy needs some manners beat into him. Maybe you should set his clothes on fire, or blow up his room. Maybe you should tie him down in the middle of the road and paint him to look like a crosswalk. I know—you can wrap his arms and his hairy little head with duct tape and make him pull it off by himself."

I knew Janis was pretty smart, but I didn't know she was demented.

"Isaac is just, well, Isaac." I said. I knew I sounded like an idiot. Actually, the tape idea was sounding pretty good. Especially since Isaac said that was my specialty. "He just can't control himself sometimes."

"Was there any truth in the things he said?"

"I didn't hear everything he told the guy from the newspaper and I didn't read the whole article so I'm not sure what the deal is, but I built the probe and I did the display and Isaac hasn't helped for months. Most of his ideas didn't work. I took them out."

"So are you done? Is the thing ready to go?" she asked. I knew that she knew a little bit about my deal with Mr. Berg, but she had been pretty cool about it up until then so I was surprised that she brought it up.

"No. It's all screwed up." I told her about the science-fair judges, especially Smiley-face-tie guy. "It won't work at all."

"What about the help you got from Ben's friend? What's his name...Wilson Pickett, Jim Pickett, what...?"

"Wilson James," I said. "He was helpful, but wrong a lot. Really wrong."

"Maybe you just didn't understand him. Go back and ask him for help."

"No," I told her. "It was a little weird there. He had me pick up after him and he didn't show up sometimes. It was just a little...weird, I guess."

"Well, maybe I can help, then. Tell me what you've got."

I showed Janis the model and the posters and told her about the places where the judges said things wouldn't work. Janis made me stop for a while until she got a pad of paper and a pencil and then she made a lot of notes. She kept asking me questions until she understood exactly what the problems were. When we were done she knew as much about the probe as I did, I guess. I don't know for sure because I can't read her writing.

Two days later Janis and Ben picked me up after school and we went to Wilson James' shop. He wasn't very happy to see us. "Kind of busy, kids. I can't help you today."

"We'd like some help with what you told Jimi," Ben said. "It looks like a lot of this won't actually work."

'You get what you pay for, and that advice was
e." Wilson James said. "That's a good lesson to
learn. Now you kids take off, okay? I really need to get
these repairs done."

I started for the door. Janis grabbed the back of my
shirt collar and pulled me back into the repair shop. I
almost fell over. "Get what you pay for, huh?" Janis
said. "How about you—do you get paid for your
work?" Wilson James looked up from his workbench.
"My brother did a lot for you, and you blew him off,
didn't you?" Now she was starting to yell. "But you
think he's just a kid, so he doesn't matter, right?" Full-
on yelling, now. I was a little scared. Ben was about to
make a run for it.

Wilson James looked a little spooked, too. But Janis
didn't budge. And she wouldn't let me move, either.
"Look," Wilson James said, finally, "I did the best I
could, okay? Seems to me that most of it would have
worked out pretty good. Why don't we all calm down,
and we'll go through it. You're right; your brother did a
good job for me. I need to do a good job for him."

Ben took a deep breath, like he hadn't breathed for a
while. I didn't know what to do. I'd never heard
anything like this before.

Wilson James walked over to the refrigerator and
got out a diet orange soda. "Show me what you got."

Chapter 13:
Space is Big

It turns out that most of what Wilson James told me was okay, as far as it went. It's just that Mars is very, very far away. Janis helped me do some calculations that showed it would take about a hundred years or so for my probe to reach Mars, if I got a big-enough push from the launcher to get the probe out of earth's orbit. I don't really understand all the math, but we asked Ms. Lipner and she thought it looked right. If it took that long to get to Mars, then everything else didn't work either because the batteries wouldn't last long enough, or there wasn't enough power to run the radio or the control system, or the whole thing got too big.

In order to make anything work, we had to get to Mars faster. Little rocket motors were not going to do it, and there was no way I could use the bigger rocket motors like in real spacecraft. They used horrible deadly chemicals and stupidly expensive metal parts that I can't get anyway.

I was pretty stuck.

Janis and Ben and Lipstick didn't have any ideas, and I wasn't going to ask Wilson James for any more help. I read some articles off the Internet, made some sketches in my math notebook, threw some paper airplanes around my room. Nothing seemed to help.

Finally, I kind of gave up for a while and concentrated on my homework. My grades were not good. Rocket science was killing me. I even helped my mom in the garden when the ground thawed out. We pulled out the old, dead plants and spread out some compost and peat moss, then shoveled the whole garden up twice to mix everything in.

"What are you going to plant this year?" I asked Mom.

"Root crops, I think. Carrots, potatoes, maybe even kohlrabi." She smiled at me over her sunglasses. "No tomatoes, though. That experiment failed."

I remembered that we bombed her fence last fall and started to apologize, but she had raised her eyes and was looking at something behind me.

"Speak of the little devil," she said.

I turned to look at what she was looking at. Sure enough, Isaac was coming through the gate into our yard. I hadn't talked to him since he got his name in the paper. I didn't really want to talk to him now.

"That's a fine-looking garden, Mrs. Peterson!" Isaac seemed to have no idea that he was the last person in the world that would be welcome in my backyard.

"Yeah, good thing you shoveled it for us," I said, "and you did a really good job pulling out all the dead plants. Why don't you wait here and I'll call the newspaper so they can send somebody over to get the story straight."

Isaac stopped walking. For the first time in his life, he looked a little hurt. "Come on, Jimi, it was just a joke. You don't need to get all bent out of shape."

So then I hit him with the shovel and crushed his skull, splattering his brains all over the garden where they could get eaten by worms, decompose and fertilize the plants. Actually I didn't move. Mom sprang into action.

"Isaac, you need to start with an apology. Then, you two need to talk this thing through, say what you both need to say, and get past it. You've been friends too long to end like this." Mom sounded really sad. Then she walked over and hugged Isaac. She didn't let him go, either. He didn't know about the hugging back part. Finally she gave up. She put her hands on Isaac's shoulders. "Get started," she said to him while she brushed off her knees, "and make it right." Then she went into the house.

Neither one of us said very much, but we did work it out, mostly. I think Isaac knew he was a jerk, but knowing you're a jerk and admitting you're a jerk are two different things.

Eventually we ended up in my room and I showed Isaac everything that had happened with the Mars probe and the rockets being too small and the batteries not big enough and the whole trip taking too long.

"Wow," said Isaac, "bummer." After a while he went home.

It was good, I guess, to get past being mad at Isaac. We had been friends for a long time. But something else happened that was pretty weird. After Isaac left I started thinking the whole Mars probe thing through, and there was this little noise in my head. It was almost like a click or a snap, like the noise you hear when a door closes or you close the latch on a suitcase.

On our first rocket Isaac had shredded the parachute so that the rocket didn't fall too slow and get carried away by the wind. That turned out to be pretty stupid, but then I remembered a picture in the book about early space exploration that Janis had given me.

I went and got the book and thumbed through the last few pages. Sure enough, in the last section, which was called "*The Way Forward,*" there was a picture of a spaceship with a parachute. Only this time, the parachute was pulling the spaceship into space. Under the picture it said, "In the future, solar sails will power spaceships long distances. Solar wind, consisting of light and sub-atomic particles boiling off the sun, will drive spaceships to the outer planets and beyond."

I figured that since this book was pretty old, I was probably in the "future" that they were talking about. I took the book and went to find Janis.

Chapter 14:
Or, You Could Do It This Way...

It took a lot of work to get the solar sail figured out. I made a huge parachute out of this really thin plastic sheet that you normally use to cover furniture when you paint, and then I tied a bunch of strings from the edges of the parachute to the nose of the rocket. It was pretty cool because I could get rid of all the rocket motors and steering rockets, which made more room for batteries and video gear and radio gear. I still didn't really know what I needed but I figured that there was plenty of room and I could get help later, when I showed it to Mr. Berg.

Isaac came by after school and I showed him the new design. "Solar wind, huh?" He didn't seem too impressed. I showed him the drawing in the old book. "So how do you steer it?"

"You don't need to steer," I said. "Earth and Mars are on the same line from the sun. You just need to let the probe blow downwind and you will pass right through Mars' orbit. If you let it go at the right time it will run right into Mars." This was pretty cool. It felt good to know more than Isaac about something. "It's like if you're going to walk by on the street. I know that if I walk out my front door, I'll cross your path. But I need to leave my house at the right time and walk at the right speed if I want to run into you on the sidewalk."

The lights went on in the mighty Isaacbrain. "But then you need to know where I am and how fast I'm moving before you know when to leave and how fast to go."

I was impressed, actually. Janis had to explain it to me for a couple of days until I could figure it out. "That's exactly right," I said, "and I don't know that stuff. But Mr. Berg's people do and they can figure it all out later."

"Cool. Really cool. You really are a rocket scientist now."

Amazing. If Isaac was impressed it had to be a good idea.

I showed him the rest of the idea and improvements I had made. Isaac even listened for a while.

"Why do you need batteries?" Isaac finally asked.

I knew that he knew why I needed batteries—to power the radios and video systems. But I thought about it for a while. Maybe Isaac had thought of something new. Then my weird brain-clicking thing happened.

"You mean use the Sun."

"Exactly," he said. "Solar wind for power, solar energy for electricity."

Isaac did it again. Just like all those kids at the science fair with their solar cars, I could use solar cells to make the electricity I needed. No batteries required.

"Pretty good, Jimi man. We're a good team, you and me." He got up to leave, then stopped at the door. "Why don't you bring this over to my house on Saturday? My mom and dad want to see how, umm, your project is going."

I was already taking the batteries off the probe and figuring out how to mount the solar panels. "Sure," I said. "See you Saturday."

Chapter 15:
Reality Check

"Well, well," Isaac's mom was impressed. "Isaac and you have done a fine job on this space probe, Jimi."

"Yeah, I've been working on it for a long time." She looked at me. "Isaac's helped, too." She kept looking at me without changing her face. Finally she looked back at the probe laid out on her basement floor. It looked huge.

"So this is your solar sail?" Isaac's dad kicked the plastic sheet with his toe. "How did you know how big to make it?"

I grabbed my space history book and showed him the picture of the solar sail. "I just made it look like the picture," I told him.

"Hmmm" he said, with his chin in his hand.

Isaac showed them the new solar panels, and explained how he thought of them and how they replaced all the batteries. His mother was very impressed, and even kissed him on the forehead. "We're so very proud of you boys," she said, looking at Isaac.

They had a bunch more questions about the TV cameras and the radio antenna and the structure of the whole thing. Isaac explained to them all about the walking out of the house at the right time at the right speed to meet someone walking up the sidewalk. They couldn't believe his brilliance at such a clear explanation.

"This is great, men," Isaac's dad said, finally. His mom called us boys but his dad called us men. I guess everyone sees what they want to see. "It's really a good attempt."

Uh-oh. I looked at Isaac. He was grinning like his face was broken. He didn't get it.

"What do you mean?" I asked. "What's wrong with it?" Isaac stopped grinning and looked at me, then at his dad.

"Well, men, you've done a fine, fine job, especially for a couple of ki...especially since you are both still young and haven't had the education and training required to take on a project of this magnitude. But for this to be a working probe, which I understand is your goal..." he looked at Isaac, then at me, then back at Isaac, "...the sail will have to be much, much larger." He stopped, and crossed his arms, kind of leaned back a little and made himself as tall as he could. "But here's a bigger problem, boys. You need to get the sail open. The solar wind is powerful enough to push the probe through space, once you get away from the earth's gravity, but it's not powerful enough to open the parachute if the plastic sheet is all balled up."

"Told you it wouldn't work," Isaac said. "Just another stupid idea." Then he left the room. His dad patted me on the shoulder and followed him.

I didn't even react. I'd had enough of Isaac for a while. I just started packing the probe up to take home. Isaac's mom rolled up the solar sail nice and neat, wrapping the strings around the plastic sheet. She finally placed it into the big box on top of everything else I had packed.

"Jimi," she said, as I picked up the box and started for the stairs, "please don't feel bad about Isaac. We know he's rude, sometimes. He just needs to grow up a little."

I gave her a little smile.

"As Isaac gets older he'll realize that sometimes it's better to lie a little and spare someone's feelings instead of telling the truth." I though my head was exploding. She was smiling at me, like she was handing me a bowl of ice cream with sprinkles and chocolate syrup.

What could I say? I didn't say anything. I took my stuff and went home.

Chapter 16:
Playing in the Band

The space probe stayed in its box for the next few weeks. It got covered with my dirty laundry twice. What else could I do? If the solar sail wouldn't work, then what? Nothing, that's what.

May finally rolled around. Mr. Berg wanted the probe on the first of June, but I didn't have any ideas. I had spent almost everything he gave me, too, plus I owed him the money that I spent on food and junk last fall.

The second week of May our band went to a festival in another town. We were supposed to play for some famous musicians and then they would tell us how to get better. It was set up like a competition, which we all thought was pretty dumb. We play for art and beauty.

Jimi & Isaac 3a:

It was a long bus ride and we were all tired by the time we got there. We had hamburgers for dinner and then we went to the gymnasium where we all would sleep. There were three other schools from out of town sleeping there, too, so it was pretty crowded. They had all the girls sleep at one end of the floor and all the boys sleep on the other end, except there were more girls than boys so the dividing line wasn't exactly in the middle. Most of the girls and some of the boys even brought pajamas. The guys in pajamas looked pretty weird, but the girls were mostly cool looking.

Anyway, everyone had sleeping bags and some kids had air mattresses. I just had my sleeping bag but I didn't mind sleeping on the hard floor. I used my wadded up shirt as a pillow. I was watching the guy next to me getting his bed ready and I had another brain-click. As he blew into his air mattress it changed from a big ball of plastic film into a pretty stiff board-like thing.

I could hardly wait to get home and try it.

We did okay in the festival, I guess. I really don't remember. The judges said we showed great spirit, and, I think, good tone, but our tempo was "sporty." I thought "sporty" was a pretty good description of our tempo. The judges weren't that famous, either.

Chapter 17:
Plastic Wrap

I had two big tests and a bunch of homework due right after I got home so I couldn't work on the probe right away.

I finally got a whole bunch of plastic and started building the world's biggest air mattress. I had to lay it out in parts because my room wasn't anywhere big enough for the whole thing. It turned into a huge mess.

"That looks like a huge mess!" Janis said, standing in the door. I could see Ben in the hallway behind her. I threw a roll of tape at her. It was almost empty anyway, and I had more. She ducked and it hit Ben in the forehead. He never saw it coming.

"Bagging the furniture?" Ben said. Wow, they were both funny. I looked around for something else to throw.

Janis picked up the closest piece of plastic film. "This is going to Mars, too?"

I explained the air mattress idea. They both got it right away.

"You need a bigger place to work," Janis said. "There's no way you can do this without laying the whole thing out."

I gave her my best stink-eye. "Duh."

Then there was a little bell-jingling noise. Ben was still standing in the hall, but he was shaking a little key ring in his hand. "This might help," he said with a big smile on his face, "...keys to the gym."

Keys to the gym did help, so we loaded everything into Janis' car. We stopped off on the way and got a fresh supply of plastic film and tape. Ben found this really, really thin film that was way lighter than the plastic I was using, and some cool tape that was sticky on both sides.

"I've got an idea," he said as we pulled into the high-school parking lot, "if you want some input?"

I figured out that he was asking me if I wanted his help. Wow. I mean, yeah, of course I want his help. I finally said, "If you have an idea you might as well say what it is."

"What if you just made an inflatable doughnut, then stretched one layer of film across it? The doughnut should be enough to support the thing in zero gravity."

Genius. He was exactly, exactly right. "Seems worth a try," I said.

He opened the gym and we spent the whole day building the world's biggest plastic doughnut and then covering it with the world's biggest sheet of plastic. Ben was great; I couldn't believe he worked so hard. Janis was cool, too.

Chapter 18:
Delivery

"Hello. Mr. Berg, please. This is Martin Peterson." The lady on the other end sounded like she was probably a teacher. She had that kind of voice that sounded nice but you knew that you had to watch what you're saying. Then I heard a click and someone picked up another phone.

"Yeah, Jimi. How are you? How's the saxophone playing?

"Great, Mr. Berg, we just went to a festival a few weeks ago."

"Super, super. Terrific, terrific." I could hear papers crinkling on his end. "Look, Jimi, I'm a little busy. What can I do for you?"

"It's finished, Mr. Berg."

"What's finished, Jimi? I don't understand...."

"The Mars probe, Mr. Berg. It's all done. I really think you're going to like it, too. It fits into two five-gallon buckets, like you said, and it weighs a little more than 100 pounds but that's because I made a few parts a little too heavy, so I can fix that, and it uses a solar sail so it doesn't need rockets...."

I heard a huge crash on his end of the phone and some kind of alarm went off, like a police siren but different.

"Look, Jimi, that's great, that's great, but I'm really kind of busy right now. I read about your science project in the paper and I hope someday you can show it to me, but really, I don't have time for this." People were shouting at his end, now. Mr. Berg covered the phone, but I could tell there was some shouting going on. "Jimi," he came back on, "I'm going to have to get back to you." And he hung up.

And that was the end of the Mars probe project.

Chapter 19:
Pizza

The rest of the week went pretty normally, really, even though I wasn't a rocket scientist anymore. I had a vocabulary test and had to write a report for history, and then I hauled the boxes with the Mars probe into the backyard, piled them up, soaked them with gasoline and burned the whole thing. The fire spread to our house and then to the neighbors. Eventually the whole town burned down and we all had to move into the school cafeteria and sleep on cots and eat canned food.

Actually, I just put the probe back in the corner of my room and started burying it in dirty laundry again.

Saturday morning I got up early and made my instant oatmeal. Janis complained about the noise I was making so I played with the microwave controls and made it ding a few extra times.

I had just settled in front of the TV when the doorbell rang. Nobody I know rings the doorbell. We're lucky if they knock.

"Jimi," Mom called, "somebody to see you." And there was Mr. Berg. Great. Just the guy I wanted to talk to.

"Why don't you men talk in the kitchen?" Mom said, to get me off the sofa. "Ash, would you like a coffee?"

I eventually made it to the kitchen table, and Mom slid a cup in front of Mr. Berg. "There's more in the pot," she called over her shoulder as she walked off, "I'll be in the garden."

We sat quietly for a while. I eventually got up and made myself a hot chocolate because it seems like if one person is drinking something then both people should drink. It's like balance or something.

"Sorry about the other day," Mr. Berg finally said. "We had a rocket fuel leak. It made quite a mess."

"Yeah," I said, sipping my hot chocolate, "that's why I got rid of the rocket engines on my probe. Strictly solar sails for me. No batteries either, only solar power. Much cleaner and lighter."

Mr. Berg started to laugh a little, and then he looked at me and saw I wasn't smiling. He looked down and took a sip of his coffee. I could tell it was too hot and it burned him a little.

"That sounds pretty innovative," Mr. Berg said, finally. "Can you show it to me?"

I almost told him that I had burned the whole thing. "Sure," I said, "let me go get it."

By the time I had hauled the last box into the kitchen Mr. Berg was already pulling the sail out of its bucket. "Don't mess that up," I said, "or we'll never get it untangled and back in."

Mr. Berg put his hands in the air like I was pointing a gun at him or something. "You're the inventor. Show me."

It took a while because I didn't have a display prepared with posters and models and when I tried to give him my science-fair speech a lot had changed so I had to start again and backtrack. I finally got through the whole thing, mostly.

"Wow," he said, getting up to pour his third cup of coffee. "That's really something. You did all this yourself, just in the last year?"

I told him the whole story. Except how Isaac is the biggest jerk in the world.

He looked at his watch. "Want to go to lunch at the plant? Maybe you can show your probe to some of the guys."

Mom said it was okay so we loaded the probe boxes into the back of his truck. Mr. Berg thought I should put on some shoes and wear a button-down shirt. I decided I might as well put on a clean pair of pants, too.

In the car Mr. Berg made a phone call. I couldn't hear everything he talked about but it was something about engineers and conference room and pizza. Sounded pretty official.

At the plant we got some help with the boxes and we had to carry them past all these really messy desks and into a conference room, which was a pretty big room with chairs along the wall everywhere and a white board at one end and a big long table down the middle. There were three stacks of pizza boxes on the table.

We put the Mars probe at one end of the table near the white board. Mr. Berg told me to tell everyone about the probe, just like I'd told him. Then he told me that if I wanted any pizza I better grab some right now.

The first box I opened was a Canadian bacon and pineapple pizza, which isn't my favorite but is good enough. I grabbed a slice and a paper towel to put it on and went to start un-packing the probe.

A horn, like a train horn, went off in some other part of the building. I looked at the clock and it was noon so I figured that was like a lunch bell.

All of a sudden the room was completely full of people. The pizza boxes were spread out and opened and the pizza was practically gone almost instantly. One really skinny guy grabbed two pieces at once and folded them together, like a sandwich. Then he ate the whole thing and reached for two more slices.

Somebody brought in bottled water and soda pop and passed them around. Passed like footballs.

It all settled down pretty quickly once the pizza was gone. The boxes disappeared off the table and Mr. Berg came over and stood next to me. He still had pizza in his hand. Sausage and pepperoni, I think.

"This is my friend Jimi," he started.

"Hellooooo, Jimaah," said a few guys on my right. They were laughing and elbowing each other. Just like the guys at the back of the room at school.

Mr. Berg just waited. "Last fall I gave Jimi a pretty big job. Way too big of a job for a kid. He surprised me. I think he will surprise you, too. I asked him to design and build a Mars probe to be launched from our rocket. I gave him size and weight limitations and a budget to work from."

The pizza-burger guy on the right had finished his lunch. "You gave him money and I can't get a new computer? No wonder we're behind!"

"I gave him less money than we spent on pizza today," said Mr. Berg, which freaked me out a little. "And now I would like you all to earn that pizza by listening to my friend Jimi." He said "friend" in a way that made me feel pretty good.

I stood up and went through the probe design. I did a lot better than when I explained it to Mr. Berg, so I guess a little practice does help, and he helped me in a few spots. By the time I was done the whole thing was spread out on the full length of the table and there was pizza sauce on the solar sail.

I stopped for a minute and everyone looked up, even the guys that were writing in their notebooks or whispering to each other in the back. I noticed a few people had left the room. We all kind of looked at each other.

Then I remembered. "Any questions?"

An old guy on the left side of the table said, "You're the kid in the paper, right, that won the science fair?" I nodded. I hope he didn't want to talk about Isaac. "Well this is a great thing," he said. "Can you continue to improve it and enter it again next year?"

"Well," I said, glancing at Mr. Berg. He didn't help. "I can, but hopefully this one will be on your rocket by then and on the way to Mars."

Apparently that was not the answer they expected, and it got a little noisy. Three guys got up and left, mumbling about "work to do," and the pizza-sandwich guy was laughing and cackling and acting like a fool. Or maybe he was acting like I was a fool. I don't know. Anyway, everyone was laughing and talking loudly and there were a couple of guys who seemed pretty upset.

I looked over at the old guy that asked me the question. He was leaning away from me talking to the two people next to him. Then they all leaned over the table and started talking to the people across the table. I couldn't hear what they were talking about because things were pretty loud.

Finally Mr. Berg stood up and banged on the table like you knock on a door. "All right, all right. It's about time to get back to work. I think you all need to join me and thank my friend Jimi here for all his hard work on this project and we can all look forward to great things from him in the future."

Then he looked at me with a great big smile on his face and reached out, like he wanted to shake my hand.

Jimi & Isaac 3a:

I knew he meant to be nice but I guess now I knew the truth. The Mars probe was just kid stuff, and I was just a kid.

Chapter 20:
Go Big or...

"Just wait a minute," said the old guy. "I may have another question or two."

"Yes, John." Mr. Berg turned towards the old guy.

The old guy waited until the room got quiet. It didn't take that long, really. "Jim, are you still in school?"

I looked at Mr. Berg. He nodded back. "Yes, sir. Two more weeks."

The old guy looked around at the people he'd been talking to. They each gave him a little nod.

"What is your full name, Jim?"

I was freaking out a little. "It's Jimi, Jimi Peterson, sir."

The room got loud again for a while, with pizza-burger guy laughing like a monkey.

The old guy just sat there for a while until the people got quiet.

"We'll need a desk and a badge for Mr. Peterson," he said to Mr. Berg. Then, "I'll get the lawyers started on the patent applications on Monday. Everyone spend the rest of today and Monday making lists of what needs to be re-worked, and Tuesday afternoon we'll get together and create a work plan."

Now everybody was yelling. It was like a second-grade recess or something. Pizza-sandwich guy was yelling really loud about his vacation time. He finally left, still yelling. It took a long time but finally things quieted down.

"Look, John," said Mr. Berg, "I'm as proud of the kid as anybody, but we're really behind schedule now. There's no way to get this into the project and still make the launch date."

"Two things, Ash," said the old guy. "First, we need to reduce our momentum to break our orbit and re-enter the earth's atmosphere, right? We throw this thing towards Mars, the probe goes fast, our capsule slows down, and everything works out. Second, you pulled me out of retirement to do something really, really great. I could be sitting on the beach with my missus right now, but I think that…umm, I think that Jimi has a great idea here and we could have a lot of fun with this thing."

I didn't really understand the momentum part, but talking about having fun seemed really weird.

Mr. Berg looked around the room. "You all on board with this?"

I noticed that the people left in the room were mostly the older people. They all nodded. The old guy spoke up, "Look, Ash, you know my rule: Go big or go home. Let's go big."

I started to giggle. Mr. Berg laughed, too. "Yeah, let's go big." Then he shook my hand.

Chapter 21:
Rocket Science

I don't remember much about the last two weeks of school except I didn't totally blow it. I think my teachers cut me a little slack because they somehow knew that Mr. Berg had hired me. A lot of the kids at school stopped calling me Jimi and started calling me "Mr. Peterson," or "Mr. Peterson, Sir" or just "Sir." Sometimes they smiled when they said it and sometimes they made kind of a mean look with their eyes. Mom says that lots of people don't like to see other people get ahead. That seems kind of stupid to me. Most of the kids were pretty nice, though.

There was a law that I could only work a few hours a day since I was just a kid and I couldn't go out in the shop without one of the adult employees, but mostly it was like a real job.

It turns out the Old Guy's name is John Crawford, and he is one of the most important guys ever in the rocket business. They gave me a desk right next to Mr. Crawford's with a phone and a little basket to put papers in. The drawers were empty and I didn't have anything to put in them until this one guy gave me a box of pens and a blank notebook. He said to write everything I did or said or thought in the book and put the date on each page. I didn't do a very good job with the notebook, though. My writing never kept up with my thinking or my doing.

I spent most of the first week after school sitting in a room with three or four guys talking about the probe design and how the different parts worked and why they were a certain way and not a certain other way. After a while I got used to saying "I don't know" if I didn't know something. That was never a problem with these guys.

A lady named Susan sat in on all the meetings. She was the lawyer that was working on all the patent stuff. A patent was a way to keep other people from stealing your ideas or copying you. "But even more important," Susan told me, "is if you have a patent other people can't stop you from doing what you invented."

Susan and I spent a lot of time on each part of the probe. How did I think of it, and when did I try it, and who knows about it, and things like that. For instance, anything on the science-fair probe couldn't be patented, because I had already talked about it in public. Luckily for me and for Mr. Berg, most of that was gone anyway.

"How about the solar sail?" Susan asked. "Tell me how you came up with that."

I showed her the history of space book with the picture. "I pretty much copied it from this," I said, "so I guess it's not my idea. Does that mean we have to do something else?"

Susan looked at the picture in the book, and then looked at the copyright date inside the front cover. "Well, this book is much more than 20 years old, so any patents on that idea have expired, and now anybody can use the idea."

"So it's in the public?"

"The public domain, that's right Jimi. But, your solar sail doesn't look quite the same as this one. Maybe the difference is important."

I told her about how I saw an air mattress on the band trip, and there was a "click" in my head, which she said was really pretty common, and that I tried to build it in my room.

"That didn't work?" she asked.

"Nope, it was just a big mess. My sister and her... umm, Janis and Ben helped me buy more plastic and tape and we built it in the gym at the high school. Actually, it was Ben that thought about making a big donut tube instead of making the whole thing an air mattress– like deal."

"That's important, Jimi. Do you know Ben's last name?"

I didn't, but later she called Janis and Janis called Ben and then Ben called Susan and then both Ben and Janis had to come in and talk to Susan and Mr. Berg. In his office, with the door closed. Eventually Susan filed for a patent on the donut sail with Ben as the first inventor and Janis and me as inventors, too. If we get the patent, Mr. Berg said he'd pay all our college costs. Pretty cool.

"What about using solar cells instead of batteries?" I asked. "That was my friend Isaac's idea. It really made a big difference."

Susan smiled, then closed her notebook and looked up at me. "Jimi, one of the very first and most important uses for solar cells was to power satellites. There is absolutely nothing new about that. Your friend Isaac 'reinvented the wheel.' It happens all the time. In fact," she said, picking up my space-history book, "here are some pictures of the early satellites." She put the open book on the table and turned it to me. "All of the satellites they show have solar cells of some kind."

"Wow. I feel dumb. I should have thought of that a long time ago, then."

"Not really, Jimi," she said, closing the book. "That's why 'reinventing the wheel' is so common. You try to find a solution to a problem, and when you discover a good solution sometimes you'll find that other people have already made the same discovery. It doesn't make your solution less correct. And," she said, standing up and putting her notebook into a big red leather purse-bag-thing, "it doesn't make patent law any easier. You'd be amazed how often we find very old patents for things someone just discovered."

The rest of the summer went really fast. Mr. Crawford said my job was to watch what was happening, answer whatever questions they asked me, not get hurt, and learn as much as I could. I also got paid. A lot. Mom called it "Rocket Scientist Money," and then put it all in a special bank account for "later," whenever that is. She did use some of the money to get me a new bike and plenty of new clothes to wear to work. I tried to use some of my money to pay Janis for the solar sail plastic and tape, but she got paid for helping Susan with the solar sail patent so she didn't want my money. I tried to pay Mr. Berg for the money I spent on lunches and reeds and stuff, but he just waved his hand at me and kept walking. I guess he was busy.

One day, Mr. Crawford came by before breakfast to pick me up in his car. Mom came along with us. She rode in the front seat and I got the back seat, which was pretty small because the whole car was pretty small. And loud. Fast, too, I guess. It was red, anyway. We went somewhere on the highway and I fell asleep so I don't know where we went, but when we got there it was a huge building. Huge and grey.

"Put these on your feet, over your shoes," Mr. Crawford told me as he handed me some white paper slippers he called "booties." We had already put on these white suits over our clothes and Mom had a net over her hair. "Now wear this over your mouth and nose." He handed me and Mom paper mouth covers with a rubber band that went around our heads. "If you have to sneeze or cough leave this over your mouth and just sneeze through it."

"Will there be dangerous chemicals?" Mom asked, looking at the paper mouth cover.

"No," said Mr. Crawford, "these are to keep your saliva, tears and mucus off the equipment. We need to keep everything in the next room very clean. That's why we need to wear the bunny suits and the hair nets."

Bunny suits. I started to giggle. Mom looked pretty good in hers, for an old lady, but Mr. Crawford looked silly. Mom gave me a look and I calmed down.

We put safety glasses on and went through two sets of doors into the biggest room I've ever seen. I really couldn't see the far end of the room very well. The floor was really shiny, and the lights reflecting off of it made it look wet.

"Well, what do you think?" asked Mr. Crawford.

I had to look for a while. Finally I figured out what he was talking about. Most of the floor was covered with shiny plastic. People were moving on it with little machines in their hands. Wait…. "Is that the sail? It's big. Wow. It's big."

Mom said: "Big. Very…big."

Mr. Crawford chuckled. "Yeah, it's big. Biggest solar sail ever made. Those people crawling around on it are heat-sealing the pieces together—melting them a little bit on the edges until they stick. They'll be done later today."

"You should have asked me," I blurted out. "Ben found this really great tape that's sticky on both sides. It's way easier than what they're doing with the heat-sealing thingy."

Mr. Crawford gave a little laugh. "Yeah, that would be easier, but we can't use adhesives or other sticky materials in space. In the vacuum of space the glue comes off the tape and gets on everything else, like camera lenses and moving parts."

"It was a good idea, though, Martin." Mom patted me on the shoulder, "don't feel bad."

I shook my back and moved off a little. Patting me? "Jeez, Mom. It's no big deal. I'm learning. Engineers make mistakes all the time. That's how they learn. Right, Mr. Crawford?"

He looked at me, then at my Mom, then back at me. "Yeah, we're all still making mistakes and learning, Mr. Peterson. But the really good engineers are still nice to their mothers." Mom laughed a little.

We walked all around the entire sail. It took a while. Then Mr. Crawford showed us where they were making some really long wires with little loops on each end.

"They look like guitar strings," I said, "for the world's biggest guitar."

"That's not too far off, Jimi. This wire is made in the same factory where they make guitar string wire. It's just a little thinner and a lot longer."

"What's it for?" Mom asked.

"The wires will run from the probe to the edge of the sail," Mr. Crawford explained. "We couldn't use string like Martin did because the cold and heat of space might make the string break. Plus, the wire is smooth and stiff so it will unwind better when we deploy the solar sail."

"Quite amazing," Mom said, putting her arm around my shoulder. "We'll have to tell your father."

Mr. Crawford went over and talked to one of the people working on the strands. He came back with a little wire loop in his hands and gave it to Mom. "I hear he's quite the guitar player. I play a little myself. Bluegrass, mostly." I couldn't see his face but his eyes were smiling.

Once we got back in his little red car and on the highway, Mr. Crawford saw me snoozing in the back seat. He pulled over and put the top down. The wind and the sunshine and the noise kept me awake for the rest of the drive. Mom's hair was a disaster when we got home. It was great.

Chapter 22:
Harmony Isn't Always Good

Being a rocket scientist sure makes summer vacation go faster. I spent as much time as they would let me at the factory but eventually most of the projects got finished and the parts packed away. There wasn't much for me to do after that.

When school started up again things got back to normal pretty quickly. I got Lipstick for science again, and this year I was in jazz band. We started with a few songs that I had played before with my dad. In jazz band, though, we had to play by the notes on the page so that we all sounded good together. That was a little different than playing with Dad, where we always tried to mix it up a little.

In fact, things at the factory slowed down enough that Mr. Berg started coming by to play Friday nights. One night Dad, of all people, wanted to talk about the Mars probe.

"Ash," he started, "sound won't travel in space, right?"

"Not through space, where there's a vacuum," Ash said. "But it will travel through the air inside the spaceship just like it does here on earth. It's actually pretty loud inside a spaceship, because the structural materials all carry sound pretty well."

Dad thought for a while. "You mean the aluminum and steel in the shell will carry sounds from the rocket motors?"

"Right. And you can hear the pumps and the valves and the fluid flowing in the tubing and all the mechanical things that happen in the spaceship."

"But only if the parts are mechanically attached together." I couldn't tell what Dad was getting at.

"That's right," said Ash. "If there's a gap between the parts, the sound won't travel through the gap because the vacuum of space won't carry sound."

Dad picked up a small loop of very fine wire and held it up so we both could see it. It was the piece of wire that we were using to hold the edges of the solar sail. "How many of these are you going to use to hold the sail?"

Mr. Berg looked at me. "Twenty-two," I said.

"Are all the wires the same length?"

"Yeah, I think so," I said.

Mr. Berg said "Exactly." Then he sat down. He was looking a little nervous, "And they all join together where they attach to the probe. We'll make them shorter or longer to make the probe accelerate slower or faster, but they'll all be the same length. Exactly the same length. Exactly."

"And the same tension?" asked my Dad. Tension is how hard you pull on something.

"Yep," said Mr. Berg. Then he put down his guitar and put his face in his hands.

"What…." I didn't get it.

Mr. Berg didn't move. I looked at my Dad. He pointed at his guitar.

"See the E string on my guitar?" he asked, "the smallest, highest pitched one?" I nodded. "If I touch the string here in the middle," which he did, "I can pick the string on this end," which he did, "and the string will vibrate on both ends." It did. "That will only work if I touch the string in the middle, where the two sides are equal, or at certain other spots where the two sides are specific fractions of each other."

"Yeah," I said, "harmonics. You showed that to me a long time ago. So what?"

"Well," he said. "Let me try this. Watch the same string on Ash's guitar." Then he turned up the amp on his guitar really loud and played the same E string. I could see the E string on Ash's guitar start to vibrate. Finally Dad turned his guitar down.

"Yeah," I said "feedback. You showed me that a long time ago, too. You can use the amplifier to make the string keep vibrating, and it can get louder and louder. I still don't see...."

"Even on another guitar string, on another guitar," Ash said, quietly.

"Yeah, even on another guitar string, on another...." and I looked at the coil of wire Dad had from the solar sail. "So all 22 sail wires will vibrate the same?"

"All the same," said Ash, standing up, "and all together. Resonating and feeding back until the sail is torn apart." Then he sat down again, and put his face back in his hands.

Dad had kind of a funny smile on his face. "Maybe not." He reached over and took a wooden pencil off a music stand next to him. "Here, Ash, put the eraser right on the end of your string."

Mr. Berg cracked a big smile. "We've got a whole family of geniuses here." He put the soft pencil eraser right on the end of the high E string and plucked it. It made the right note, but it was dull and didn't ring. Dad did the same thing as before, turning his guitar way up and plucking an E. No matter how loud Dad's guitar got, the E string on Mr. Berg's guitar never moved. Dad finally turned it down.

"Heyyyyyyy!" It turns out Janis had been yelling from the basement door for a while. "People are working up here!"

"Sorry," Mr. Berg said to Janis. Then he gave my Dad a big smile. People were working down here, too. "And now I need to go make a little change in the probe. You just saved me, Jim."

Jimi & Isaac 3a:

Dad smiled and nodded his head a little, then he started working a simple little twelve-bar shuffle on his guitar. "Drop in whenever you like, my rocket scientist son," he said.

Chapter 23:
Launch

I had to miss a lot of soccer practice early in the season because I went to the launch. School was a little problem, too. Luckily most of my teachers thought that being a rocket scientist would be a good learning experience for me and so they gave me projects that had to do with the launch. For instance, my art teacher gave me a camera and asked me to take pictures and make a photo album when I got back.

Since everybody in my family was now a rocket scientist except Mom we all got to go to the launch. Mom got to go, too. And Ben. We stayed in this really nice hotel and had company badges and ate in really nice restaurants and they had video games on the TV in the hotel room. Mom and Janis and Ben sat by the pool most of the time. Dad didn't know what to do during the day but at night he would go listen to music at all the bars in town. Mom went twice but she didn't like the noise and the smoke so she just went to bed early. Mr. Berg went with Dad a couple of times too, but he was pretty busy.

On the final morning before the launch they had a press conference where the newspapers and TV people could meet Mr. Berg and Mr. Crawford and the pilot, who is called an astronaut since he is flying a spaceship. The newspaper people could ask questions and get the pictures that they needed for the paper that night.

Mom made me put on a tie while we were getting ready for the press conference. "Why?" I asked. "I'm already wearing a button-up shirt. That's fancy enough."

"Look, Martin," she said, smiling but not really smiling, "we didn't want you to get nervous or upset so we didn't tell you before, but you're in this press conference, too. You'll be up on the stage with everyone else."

So I threw up on her. All over her blouse and nicest pants. Breakfast with extra orange juice. My shirt stayed clean. Apparently I'm a very specific vomiter.

She changed into a skirt that really looked better than the pants, so it worked out okay. Dad says that Mom has great legs. I guess. Anyway, we all finally made it to the press conference. It was in a fancy room near the lobby of the hotel. There was a stage with a table and chairs and water glasses for everybody on the stage, and about a thousand TV cameras in the back and about a thousand chairs for the newspaper guys. The room was really bright. There were extra lights everywhere, especially aimed at the table on the stage. We saw Mr. Berg and Mr. Crawford over on the side.

"Come here, Jimi," Mr. Crawford said. "You don't look so good. Let me fix your tie."

"Jimi had a little upset stomach this morning," Mom said, "and I'm afraid we don't wear many ties in our family."

"That's not even a little problem," said Mr. Crawford. "If you ask the people in there...." and he nodded towards a door on the side of the stage, "they'll be glad to fix Jimi a little dry toast and ginger ale. Happens all the time around here, believe me."

Mom went off to get me the snacks. Dad went with her. Janis and Ben walked to the back of the room to look at the television cameras.

"Don't worry, Jimi, you'll do fine," said Mr. Berg.

I kind of looked down and kicked the floor a little. "I don't know...."

"Nothing to worry about, really. Just be yourself."

"What if the rocket doesn't work, what if the probe doesn't work, what if the sail doesn't open, what if...."

Mr. Crawford grabbed me by the shoulders and looked me right in the eyes. "What if you're the first kid to design and build a failed interplanetary probe? Then you're still the same kid you were yesterday. And that's pretty good. Maybe later in life, if you work really hard, you can be the first person ever to work on two failed probes. If you really, really work hard, you can work on three failed probes and have written some really bad music. You'll still be in better shape than the people that didn't try."

I saw where he was going: "Go big or…"

"…or go home," he finished. "That's right."

"You two about done?" Mr. Berg said quietly. "There's no hugging in front of the press." He was looking at the door. I turned and could see people coming in. Lots of people. Some of them looked like they'd been up all night.

The ginger ale was pretty good but I didn't eat my toast. I didn't want junk on my teeth for the TV cameras.

Mr. Berg stood and talked about the mission, and then he sat down and the press asked questions. Mostly they wanted to talk to the astronaut. They asked if he was afraid of dying, which, now that I think of it, was a pretty good question. I hadn't even thought about that part of the whole deal. I started to freak out a little. I still wasn't sure why I was there. It all seemed a little stupid, really, a dumb kid like me up here in front of all these people, just….

Then Mr. Crawford kicked my foot under the table. I looked up at him, and he was looking out into the room. It was really quiet. I looked out, too. There was a man standing up in the middle of the room wearing a blue sweater with a pad of paper in his hand.

"Perhaps you could repeat the question," said Mr. Berg.

"Sure," said the sweater man. "Mr. uhhmm, Mr. Peterson, can you tell us about the Mars probe you designed?"

I looked at Mr. Berg. He shrugged.

"Well," I said, "it's about this long (I held up my arms) and about this round (I put my hands together and made my arms into a circle) and when we launch it it will get really big and a solar sail will carry it to Mars where the gravity will pull it in and we'll crash into it just like when you walk out the door and run into it on the sidewalk."

That answer didn't even sound good to me. What a mess.

Mr. Berg came to the rescue. "Maybe you could ask something more specific."

Yeah, it was a pretty stupid question. Mr. Berg was right. Maybe they should ask a better question.

A lady in the front row stood up, and Mr. Berg pointed at her. She asked if I've always wanted to design rockets.

Finally a question I can answer. "Actually," I said, smiling, "I've always wanted to play the saxophone. Rocket design is kind of a hobby of mine."

Mr. Crawford stepped on my foot, hard. Mr. Berg put a serious smiley face on. I think it's called a grimace. "One last question, and then I think we're done."

About ten people raised their hands. Mr. Berg pointed to a man in the second row with a huge microphone. He was wearing makeup, so I guess he had some TV job.

"So is this a game, Mr. Peterson, or are you really involved with building the Mars probe?"

Wow. Something had gone really, really wrong. I wasn't sure what it was. Mr. Berg and Mr. Crawford were looking straight ahead. The astronaut was smiling a little. I think he was trying not to laugh.

"I don't know what you mean," I finally answered.

"Mr. Peterson," TV guy said, with his voice getting deeper, "did you actually build the Mars probe, or is this just some sort of publicity stunt on the part of Mr. Berg?"

The astronaut made a little noise through his nose like the not laughing wasn't working.

"I built it. I…we built it. It's not a stunt. I …."

Everyone was quiet. TV guy didn't look very happy with me.

Mr. Crawford came to my rescue. "This is a team effort. Mr. Peterson is a valuable part of our team, and he did most of the initial work on the Mars probe and has been a great help getting it ready for today's launch. No one person is completely responsible for any one part of this entire project."

TV guy wasn't done. "What exactly did he actually do?"

Mr. Crawford growled a little. I don't think anybody heard him but me.

Mr. Berg stood up. "That's all for this morning, and thank you for coming. We'll see you all after the launch."

Mr. Crawford stood, grabbed me by the elbow, and headed us both for the door to the kitchen area where Mom had gotten my ginger ale.

"Sorry about that, Jimi. We should have seen that coming. Those clowns were nasty. Are nasty. Will always be nasty."

Mr. Berg and the astronaut came through the door behind us.

"Don't worry about it, kid. Welcome to the big leagues." Astronaut was finally laughing out loud. Mr. Berg started laughing, too.

Mr. Crawford wasn't laughing. "I don't know what's so funny. They tried to lynch this kid."

"Ease up, John. Just relax. Breathe in, breathe out. The press is..., well, the press is the press. They have to have stories to sell, even if they have to make them up. We'll get a chance to tell our story later."

"Don't worry," Astronaut said, putting on his great big mirrored astronaut sunglasses. "Today they tried to ruin you. That means that tomorrow, they'll turn you into a hero." He smiled at me, and I smiled back. This guy was pretty funny. "Of course," he said, elbowing Mr. Berg, "the day after that they'll burn you down and dance on the ashes."

Chapter 24:
Real Life

The rocket launch went great. The sky was clear, with just a few really white puffy clouds. Mom said it all looked like a painting. The rocket was loud beyond anything. It wasn't even like noise. It was like being underwater.

The capsule went into orbit and went around the earth, I think, nine times. Then they used this crossbow kind of thing to shoot the Mars probe forward, flinging it out of orbit and starting it towards Mars. Shooting the probe forward slowed the capsule, making it fall out of orbit and back into the earth's atmosphere. Eventually it put out its own glider-shaped parachute called a paraglider. My new buddy the astronaut somehow steered the paraglider to land at a runway just down the road from the launch pad. He was, just like he said, a hero.

Once the probe was clear of the earth they used remote controls to inflate the solar sail and it started on its way to Mars. Everyone said it worked really well. The government even used some super-secret satellite space telescope to take a picture of it. You could see the solar sail and the wires holding the sail and the shadow of the probe right in the middle of the sail, just like you'd expect. It didn't look real. Mr. Berg made me a great big poster of the picture that I put up on my wall. He gave a copy to Lipstick, too. She put it up in the hallway outside her room. Some kids drew some Martians on it with marker but it still looks cool.

My last year in middle school went pretty normally, really, except I wasn't as good at soccer as I was last year because of all the practice I missed and I was in pretty bad shape. I really liked jazz band and actually got to play a couple of solos in our last concert. I did okay in my classes too, except in Spanish. My vocabulary tests were *bueno, más o menos*, but I couldn't figure out *los verbos*.

Five months after the launch we got this amazing picture back from the probe. Most of the picture was completely black. In the center of the picture was a white ball. That was the sun. A dot off to the left was the first planet, Mercury. A dot off to the right was the second planet, Venus. And way off to the left, almost off the picture, was a tiny little dot. That was Earth. It was a very small dot.

When it was finally time for summer vacation there wasn't much to do on the Mars probe. They had to make a few adjustments on the size of the solar sail on the way out to make sure we didn't go too fast and pass Mars on the way out but mostly it worked pretty well. Mr. Crawford spent most of the summer on a beach with his wife, in fact. Most of the rest of the guys at Mr. Berg's company were working on a newer, bigger rocket to take the communication and other satellites into orbit so they could make more money for Mr. Berg. I didn't have much to do with that. To tell you the truth, I didn't have anything to do with that.

Mr. Berg came by every couple of weeks or so to play guitar with my dad and me, and after a while Isaac started showing up, too, to play drums. He was really polite, especially to Mr. Berg.

During the summer Mr. Berg had a bunch of TV guys making a film about the Mars probe. They had actually been taking video of Mr. Berg's company for a long time. They mostly worried about the rocket and the astronaut at first, though. Mr. Berg told me not to talk to them by myself and he made sure that either he or Susan, the patent lady, was there when I talked to them. Eventually I showed them all the ideas we had and all about the science fair and the newspaper articles, and they interviewed Wilson James and took video of his shop. It was pretty cool. They never did talk to Isaac, but they did record Dad and Mr. Berg and me and Isaac playing and Isaac was drumming, so I guess that counts. We were pretty good that day, too. We was smokin'!

Chapter 25:
Blam!

"Jimi, you'll have to get someone to help you with your tie." Mom was getting agitated.

"I'll help him, Miz Peterson," said Ben. He was all dressed up in a suit already and actually had a mustache that didn't look stupid like it did last year. He and Janis were starting college in three weeks, and I was going to high school in two, so I guess we were all adults now. "There you go, Jimi, all fixed up."

"Can you help me, too, Ben?" Dad was a mess. His tie was tied in a big tangled knot and the thin part was way longer than the wide part and it was in the front. He was also wearing a brown tie with a blue and white striped shirt, which was probably not that great of an idea.

"You are not going to wear a tie," Mom said. "Come over here." She pulled the brown tie off his neck and gave him a silver and turquoise bolo tie, like cowboys wear. Simpler, but better too, I thought. More like Dad.

"Nice call, Mom," I said. Dad smiled.

Mom and Janis were totally on top of things. They actually sort of matched in these really nice flouncy white dresses with little yellow and blue flowers. Dad said they looked like a camera commercial. I think he meant it in a good way. Mr. Berg had given them both matching droopy earrings that looked like rockets with little diamond sparkles where the flames come out the back.

Somebody knocked on the hotel room door and stuck his head in. "Hurry on down, folks. Mr. Berg wants to start in about ten minutes."

Ben held out his hand to Janis and they left. Dad watched them go, then looked at Mom and made a little wiggle with his eyebrows. Then he followed them. "See you in the movies," he said.

I was putting my jacket on and Mom was making one last check of her makeup. "Wait a minute, Jimi," she said as I started out the door.

I stopped and she walked up to me and put her hands on each shoulder. She had to reach up. Then she gave me a hug. It was maybe her best hug ever; only she forgot to let go when I hugged her back.

Finally she eased up and put her hands back on my shoulders. "I don't know how many more of those I'll get," she said. Then she spun me around and pushed me out the door.

We didn't want to wait for an elevator so we ran down the fire stairs. We caught up with Dad just as he came out of the elevator. He took Mom's hand and we followed the door-shouting guy into this huge room. It was a lot like the room where we had the press conference for the launch except the carpet was mostly red instead of mostly blue, and there were two huge screens set up behind the stage with smaller TVs on the sides of the room further back. There were some newspaper people and TV people, but most of the people in the room were from Mr. Berg's company. Pizza-sandwich guy gave me the thumbs-up.

"Up you go," said Mom, waving me towards the stage. "We'll see you when it's over."

I took my seat at the table. The astronaut guy wasn't there but Mr. Crawford was, and he had a really good tan. In fact, the top of his head was red and peeling where he was bald. "Good to see you, Jimi," he said, "I got you a ginger ale."

I laughed. Mr. Crawford was a good guy. "Don't worry, no barfing today," I said.

Mr. Berg got up and said some stuff, and then they dimmed the lights and put video up on the big screens. We actually couldn't see very well because the screens were practically straight above us.

"The shot on the left is from NASA," Mr. Berg said. "They were kind enough to give us a live feed directly from the orbiting planetary observatory. It's a wide shot of Mars. The screen on the right is the live video feed from the camera on board our Mars probe. It's black because Mars hasn't come into the picture yet. Basically that camera is pointed into deep space right now."

He got a wave from a guy that was on the phone offstage.

"Great," Mr. Berg said, "we just got the signal that we will reach Mars in one minute. Very soon Mars will show up on the Probe video and the probe will show up on the Mars video. The probe will hit the surface of Mars at about forty thousand miles per hour, so this will happen pretty quickly. Please pay close attention."

Mr. Crawford and I got out of our chairs and walked around to the front of the stage so we could see the screens above us. They were still too high, so we climbed down off the stage and went to the side of the room, more towards the back. We ended up pretty close to where Mom and Dad were sitting.

"Ok," said Mr. Berg, "Ten more seconds. "At five seconds left we should just start to see the probe in the picture of Mars…there it is!"

There was the tiniest flash of light on the left side of the picture of Mars, moving very fast towards the middle of the screen. There was one flash of non-black on the Probe camera, and then the picture disappeared. At the same time the bright dot on the video of Mars went away.

I started to laugh. So did a few other people. "That was it?" I asked Mr. Crawford. "All our work for that? Wow."

Mr. Crawford put his finger to his lips and then pointed to Mr. Berg.

"If we just wait a moment, NASA should have a close-up replay for us. Remember that the probe was traveling very, very quickly. If Mars had much of an atmosphere the probe would have burned up like a meteor before it hit. Hopefully, we'll soon have...."

The picture of Mars flickered a little, and we couldn't see the ball of it anymore, just reddish-brown with a few craters. There were numbers in the four corners of the picture, too. I found out later they were the location of the probe impact and the time.

"Okay, okay, okay." Mr. Berg was getting a little excited. "Now they'll play the impact back in slow motion. If we just wait a little, they'll play it...."

There was a flash from the left side of the picture and then there was a little puff of dust on the surface of Mars.

"Wow, wow, did everyone see that?" They were playing it again. Mr. Berg was looking at the phone guy offstage. "Can they zoom in some more?" Phone guy was talking on the phone. He nodded at Mr. Berg.

The picture jumped again and now all we could see was bright red dirt and the very edge of a crater. The shadows were really, really dark. It didn't look real.

"Okay, okay, they're zooming in some more. Now watch the right si...."

Blam! I mean, there wasn't any sound, but the surface of Mars just exploded. It looked like the biggest movie explosion ever. You could tell it was huge. I started jumping up and down. NASA was playing it over and over. Even Mr. Crawford was worked up. He had his hands up over his head and was doing a little dance.

Mr. Berg jumped off the stage and grabbed the phone from the phone guy so he could talk to whoever was on the other end. In the meantime, NASA replayed the explosion in super slow motion and then super-duper slow motion. You could see the probe come into the picture and see the solar sail and then it hits Mars and disappears and then this great big dust cloud shoots up and away from where the probe hit. Everybody in the room was screaming. It was great.

Mr. Berg gave the phone back to the phone guy and jumped onto the stage. "Okay, okay, okay, okay. They're pretty excited back there at NASA, too," he said. People quieted down a little. "All the analysis is pretty preliminary, and the probe hit about 150 miles from where we thought it would. It made a hole about..." I think he did some math in his head, "...about a quarter of a mile long. They detected water and ice in the debris plume, too, and they didn't know there was water there, so we've already made a significant discovery!"

Things just got better from there. Apparently nobody noticed or cared that the video camera on the probe was pretty worthless. If it worked at all we were just going too fast. The press took some pictures and talked to Mr. Berg and Mr. Crawford and me and Mom and Dad, but nobody asked any stupid questions. The people from the company were real happy and came over and told me "good job" and "way to go." Then there was a bunch of food and a band. Dad and Mr. Berg ended up playing with the band later on (they called the song "Running into Mars," but it was really just a straight 12-bar blues shuffle with solos), and I even saw Janis and Ben dancing together on a slow song. I saw Mr. Crawford dancing with his wife, too. It was quite a night.

Chapter 26:
This Ain't Rocket Science, You Know

The high-school principal made a big deal about the whole thing on my first day of school. That wasn't so great, if you know what I mean. Sometimes you want to start things a little slower. We had an assembly where the mayor of the town came to give me a plaque. The whole school met me as a famous rocket scientist instead of a pretty good saxophone player or an okay math student. I guess it could have been worse.

Then it got worse. After the assembly the same newspaper guy from two years ago was there to take my picture. The mayor shook my hand while he handed me the plaque again and we both smiled. After the newspaper guy took his picture I tried to make a break for it.

"Mr. Peterson," the newspaper guy yelled, "can I ask you a few questions?"

I was almost out of earshot, but not quite. I stopped, and then turned and walked back. "Sure," I said.

"Look," he said, "I know I was wrong about you before. I was trying to write a certain kind of story, and I should have dug a little deeper. It's obvious now to everybody that you really are the designer and builder of the first privately built spacecraft to ever travel from Earth to Mars. The scientists at NASA tell me that your probe uncovered a huge ice and mineral deposit that they hadn't found before, and that what you've done is one of the most important things that ever happened in the advancement of space travel. You're a hero. I'd really like to get your side of the story, and I'll let you tell it yourself. Would that be all right?"

I looked at him for a long time, and then nodded. He got out his note pad and a pen and looked up at me.

"Ready when you are," he said. "Start whenever you like."

I took a deep breath. He still had his story wrong. I would have quit right away except Lipstick stuck me in the science fair. That led to Wilson James and all his crazy ideas that led to some crazy ideas of my own, and without Ben and Janis the solar sail wouldn't have ever worked. If Dad hadn't figured out the whole harmonic vibration thing then the probe would have torn itself apart in space. All the stuff I built was kind of goofy. Mr. Crawford and the other guys made the real probe that really worked. Even Isaac was more help than he ever got credit for. I wasn't a hero. All I did was keep going.

I took another deep breath. No way I could explain all this stuff. No way.

Newspaper guy just waited.

"I had a lot of help," I said. "A lot." Then I turned and went to class.

END

Phil Rink is a Professional Mechanical Engineer, inventor (with eleven patents so far), entrepreneur, and science team and soccer coach. He's published a book on sailing the Caribbean, several magazine articles, and a few professional papers.

He lives with his family in the upper left-hand corner of the United States of America.

Made in the USA
Lexington, KY
09 November 2010